Face the Music

First Paperback Edition Mar 2024

979-8-9902083-0-8

Published by Stephanie Jean | Birdcage Ink
www.Birdcageink.com

Face the Music

Stephanie Jean

1 - Connie - Now

One thing about working for Lillian: she's always moving. Maybe that comes with the territory of chasing your dreams in a highly competitive industry, but maybe it's just her.

"They're almost here!" I shout through the condo. How Lilli ever manages to get places on time, I'll never really know.

It's a big day, and I'm a little groggy from not being able to sleep last night due to the excitement. We're both still riding the wave of becoming "internet sensations" this past year. Yes, I include myself in that, even though I'm not the one in the spotlight. I mean, I wrote the lyrics to her hit song, "Salutations", after all. Most people don't look at the credited writers, though—just the name of the singer.

Lillian, Lilli to me, has tried to convince me to release music myself, but I'm fine where I'm at. I write songs for people to hear, and they're listening. Why would I change anything?

Luckily for me, Lilli and I are best friends, have been for almost a decade, roommates for half of that. We were even in a band together for a while — Scarlet Sofa. Then, life happened. Things change, and now, I'm writing songs and occasionally acting as Lilli's assistant. I love that girl, but she'd forget her head if it wasn't attached. I've been her assistant of sorts for a long time, but that's just my love language, taking care of her in the ways I can—making sure she stays on schedule, keeping her away from trolls online.

Wouldn't everyone do that for their best friend? I love being here for her, and I know she's grateful for it—she tells me so all the time. Of course, I know she doesn't really need me to do it all; she's grown and can do it herself. She writes songs herself too, so I guess there's a part of me that feels a need to show her my value, like if I don't, she might realize she doesn't need my songs either.

The craziest thing that has come out of this is being considered by Ripple Records, the record label founded by international popstar Jennifer Lux. Lilli has been chosen as an opening act for Jennifer's tour.

I remember the night we applied. We'd just finished going through a spring-cleaning checklist; Lilli is a real material girl, as Madonna intended. We were on a Marie Kondo kick when Lilli turned to me and said, "You know what would spark joy? Performing in stadiums."

Then, she handed me her phone with the application open. We recorded the self-tape that night, using her most popular track. It's a sad break-up song, one about when she got a matching tattoo with a girl who wrecked her like a tornado.

Lilli is going on tour with Jennifer Lux for three weeks, and Ripple Records said she could bring her own assistant, so, voila: here I am.

Ripple Records sent a car to pick us up; it's black and big, and I'm honestly the worst with cars. "This is a real step up from the Buick," Lilli says quietly to me, referring to the old car she's had since college.

"Hey, that dusty old thing got us where we needed to go."

She grins as we start moving. "This is absolutely insane, right?"

I nod in agreement. "I feel like we're in *The Princess Diaries*. You know, that scene with the limo?

"This is a lot cooler than a limo," the driver says. He's a big guy, in muscle, height, *and* tattoos, surprisingly alternative and punk rock for a driver.

"What's your name?" Lilli asks.

"Ash Robinson. I'll be your security detail, Ms. Davis."

"Please, call me Lilli."

"Alright, Lilli. Ms. Abram, would you like me to call you Constance?"

I make a face. "Connie is fine, thanks."

When we arrive at the lot, there's a tour bus waiting for us. Ash comes around to open our door, and as he makes his way around, Lilli grabs my hand. We give little squeals of glee, stopping as soon as the door opens. Lilli exits the car, forgetting her phone behind, but I notice as I leave and grab it for her.

In the lot, the tour bus looms large. There are dozens of people running around, toting guitar cases, sound boards, amps, and boxes, all labeled with their placement and owner. Some people have walkie-talkies, while others are so focused, they don't even look our way as they load up equipment.

A small woman with a loud voice rushes forward. "Hello, I'm Topanga, but everyone calls me Tops," she says with the rasp of a heavy smoker. She shakes Lilli's hand and then mine, and I notice that, despite her voice, she doesn't smell like cigarettes. "I'm the assistant tour manager for Luxury Tour."

No nonsense, right to business, Tops has the energy of someone with a long to-do list, but she's one hundred percent going to accomplish it before going to bed tonight.

"Lillian, come meet your hair and makeup crew. They'll be traveling separately, but they'll be at the shows. They want to do a toxicity test."

"A what?" Lilli asks, but Tops doesn't seem to hear as she leads us away.

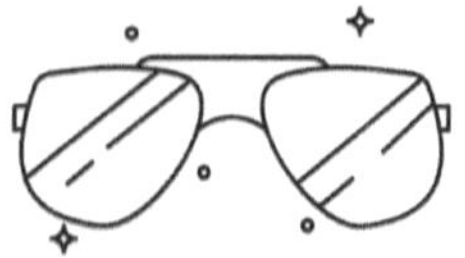

2 – Eric – Now

I thank my rideshare driver for the lift and grab my duffle bag from the trunk with a grin. I can see the tour bus from here.

"Is that for the Luxury Tour?" the driver asks, and I cringe. I hope he isn't a fan. "My daughter loves her."

"Isn't Jennifer Lux performing in a different state right now?" I say, hoping to dissuade him from prying further.

"I can't keep up with all that," he says with the classic tired dad mentality. "It's her thing. I just recognize the name."

Obviously, he would recognize the name of the highest-grossing musician of our, well, *my* generation.

"Well," he continues, "don't forget to rate me. If you had a good trip, five stars helps a lot. Stay smart out there."

"Yes, sir. Thanks again." I close the door to his Toyota Camry and watch him drive away before I check my surroundings—about a dozen people are packing up things that look like sound equipment and cables. I unlock my phone and call my buddy, Ash.

"Hey man," he greets me when he answers.

"I'm here; where do I go?" Just as I finish my sentence, I see him. Ash is a few inches taller than me; he looks like he either works under a car or swings an axe, his tattoos and beard confirming he's the right big guy. "Never mind, I see you."

"Good to see you, Eric." Ash and I give each other a big bear hug as we meet in the middle of the lot.

"You too. Man, I really appreciate you calling me. I needed the work."

"Of course. Your family is like family to me." He takes a hit off his vape. "Just don't tell your mom I'm still doing this." He gestures to the vape pen. "She'd kick my ass."

I let out a laugh—he's right.

Just then, a short woman interrupts our reunion. "Ash, I'm not paying you to have a good time." She stops in front of me, and she's so close, I have to angle my head down to look at her. "Who's this?"

I look at Ash, the question clearly directed at him.

"Eric Stone, the guy I called to fill in for Gary," Ash explains.

"Background check?" the woman asks.

"Done and clear," Ash responds.

"Hmm." She crosses her arms and looks me over like I'm a piece of meat at a butcher's mart and she's a paying customer, wanting the best cut. "Well, welcome to the US leg of the Luxury Tour. My name is Tops, and my job is to make sure nothing goes wrong. Your job is to keep the opening act safe. You'll be paired with Ash on that. You two are the personal guards: one for the singer—that's you, Ash," Ash nods, "and you'll be on the personal assistant. They're a close pair, so it should be easy enough."

She looks at me with that measuring gaze again, and I nod. She makes me feel uneasy like she expects me to drag mud through a freshly mopped house. It's like I'm in trouble before I even did anything. I roll my shoulders back; I won't disappoint her or Ash. I have too much at risk.

Tops must be impressed by me not backing down from her gaze, because she gives Ash an approving nod. "This one seems good."

"Have I ever let you down?" His smile tells me that no, he hasn't.

Tops shakes her finger at him. "Don't start. Anyway, this is the bus you two will be on with Lillian and Constance."

I swear, my heart squeezes, the whole organ off-rhythm now. This has to be a coincidence, right?

3- Connie – Then

The southern California desert was windy. You might expect it—they show it all the time in those old western movies, a single tumbleweed blowing lazily by, the only movement in a tense situation. This wind, however, felt more like an incessant toddler, demanding attention because it knows no other form of communication. It whipped my hair around my face, strands sticking to my lip gloss like flies in a spider's web. If there was a ranking of sensory icks, hair in lip gloss had to be number one.

I got in Lilli's old Buick and pulled down the visor to look in the mirror. With a brown napkin from the glove box, I wiped the lip gloss off as thoroughly as possible.

"Okay, drive safe." Lilli's dad was saying his goodbyes and checking the oil in the car before we took off. "Don't forget to change your clock when you cross over the state border."

"Why?" Lilli questioned. "We never did that before."

"The time change," her mom said casually, holding her little white puffball of a Pomeranian. "They don't do daylight savings time in Arizona, so they're an hour ahead." My mouth was hanging open, and my heart felt like it got a kick start.

"Shit!" Lilli said. "We have to leave!"

Her mom gave her *the look*. "Language, please."

"Sorry, Mom. Bye! Love you guys!" Lilli slammed her door and started the engine.

"Drive safe!" her dad reiterated.

"Thank you!" I called out to her parents as Lilli booked it out of the cul-de-sac.

"Shit, shit, shit," Lilli muttered as she navigated toward the freeway. "Can you put the address in?" She handed me her phone, and I punched the address of the hotel into the navigation app.

"We're going to be about fifteen minutes late," I explained. "But it's mostly freeways and highways, so we might be able to shave a few minutes off." I was grateful I had remembered to make us tea before we left and that our reusable water bottles were filled. We had some protein bars that were supposed to be a snack for later in the day, but they'd have to do for breakfast.

"We have about an hour of driving, so vocal rest for twenty minutes, then we'll check in and do some warmups."

We listened to a podcast on the way across state lines. I needed to get my nervous energy out. I tried applying lip balm, since I couldn't get myself to trust lip gloss yet again, and then I picked at my nail polish and instantly regretted it. The idea of having ugly nail polish on while on stage started to freak me out, only adding to the anxiety of possibly being late to the festival, so I tried my best to make it uniform. My hair was charged with static electricity from rubbing against the cloth headrest of the seat. I took some water from my water bottle and ran it through my hair, praying it would appease the frizz. I contemplated putting my hair up, but I didn't want to risk it creasing and then going on stage with a ponytail crease in my hair.

"Shit," Lilli broke the silence, and I see that she rubbed her eye and smeared her eyeliner along her face and hand. "Can you get me a wipe? I need your help," she says as she starts cleaning off one eyelid.

I took the wipe and cleaned off the smudges of black eyeliner that had migrated closer to her ear.

"My makeup is in the blue bag."

I stared at her. "You can't put on makeup while driving!"

"I won't be putting it on—*you* will be putting it on for me." She was explaining it to me like it was obvious, that I should have already understood the solution.

Thankfully, the road was pretty empty—just the occasional semi-truck in the slow lane on a two-way, east bound highway, the other side separated from us by a wide desert strip.

"Fine," I agreed. I twisted in the passenger seat and grabbed her blue makeup bag before I started applying some peach-colored eyeshadow to her eyelid. I added some white shimmer before I climbed into the back seat to do the other eye. "You'll have to forego eyeliner or apply it yourself when we stop. Same for mascara. I'm not going to be responsible for your eye getting stabbed."

"I can do the mascara," she said, taking the pink and green tube from me. "We're only about five minutes late now, which may or may not be the result of completely ignoring the speed limit. Oh, don't give me that face. We're fine."

I rolled my eyes. "About to get fined, you mean."

Lilli waved her hand, mascara wand still in her grasp. It kind of hit me right then how dangerous the last few minutes had been, and I burst out laughing.

"Dude, let's never do that again."

Lilli started laughing with me —honestly, we sounded a bit unhinged and slightly manic.

"One day, when we're being interviewed for the Rolling Stones magazine or something, they're going to ask us 'what's the craziest thing you've ever done', and this is going to be the story we tell."

"And they'll be expecting something about drugs or partying," I interjected.

"But we are completely sober!"

"Naturally reckless and stupid."

"Naturally."

I opened my notes app on my phone and started jotting down some thoughts.

Driving the interstate

Putting on warpaint flawless,

A Bonnie and Clyde kind of reckless

Maybe one of these would end up good enough for a lyric, or maybe they'd die in the notes app. No one ever really knew.

We arrived at the hotel hosting AAF – American Artist Festival – this year to find the parking lot full, and we made a lap, anxieties peaking. I nearly screamed when I saw a car backing out, and Lilli whipped the car in and threw it in park. I grabbed our guitars and she grabbed our purses, and we ran.

There were three registration tables with white tablecloths, but they condensed down to one since nearly everyone else was already there. The silver lining, though, was that there wasn't a line. The lady behind the table, who had to be in her eighties, begrudgingly greeted us. Her under-the-eye black eyeliner was smudged, and it looked harsh paired with her perm and navy blue cardigan.

"Scarlet Sofa, music division."

She handed us our lanyards with our competition number—9A. "Go through those doors," she pointed to a conference room at the end of the lobby, "and a stagehand will be with you soon."

We thanked her and speed-walked into the room she indicated. As soon as we walked in, as if the stars had perfectly aligned, a stagehand in all black joined us.

"Hello, Group A! We have a slight delay, as guests from the other divisions are getting seated and arriving. Please get yourselves lined up in numerical order, starting with 1A here at the door and 15A back towards that wall. I'll be back in a few minutes!"

Everyone adjusted according to their badge numbers as we found our spot between 8A, a woman who gave major Joan Jett vibes, and 10A, a group of wannabe Beach Boys. An interesting and diverse line-up; I wondered if they intentionally blended different genres of music, or if it was just random. I imagined what the other groups must have thought of us. We're both wearing cream with peach accent pieces, very *same outfit different fonts*. Hers was more Lana Del Rey, trying to give that old money feel in a cute little dress an empire waist. The fabric was printed with a soft peach floral pattern so opaque, it blended into the cream background. She paired it with peach socks and peach Mary Jane platforms, her honey-brown hair pulled back half-up with two little braids. I, meanwhile, went for a more modern pop look: a cream-white pantsuit and peach bodice instead of a shirt and my peach-colored boots. I decided to put my hair up in a slick ponytail – or as slick as I could get it, since the gel was still in the car.

With deep breaths, we went through our preshow ritual of listing the things we had going in our favor.

"We're on time," Lilli said, her smile mischievous.

"We look great." I pointed at her eyeshadow.

"Guitars are tuned."

"Vocal warms are done."

"Songs are rehearsed."

"And the things out of our control aren't worth worrying about."

"Because we can't do anything about them anyway."

"And if anything comes up, we can adapt as needed," I finished.

Lilli pulled me in for a big hug. "I'm so fucking glad you're here."

The door opened, and the room that had been quietly buzzing fell quiet.

"Alright everyone," the returned stagehand announced, "are you ready?" Everyone nodded as they straightened out the line. "Follow me."

Lilli and I cheered using our guitar pics in our favorite colors (mine yellow, hers pink). I tried to ignore that nervous feeling in my stomach —it was definitely excitement instead of anxiety. I thought about escaping quickly to the bathroom; I still carried a blade in my pocket, even though I hadn't used it in a while. The urge for release pulled at me, but I brushed it off as Lilli held my hand and smiled.

I couldn't let her down.

4 – Connie – Now

He comes over in powerful strides. It's definitely Eric, but he's different. For one, he's filled out, muscles where there had been lean limbs. What was slender is now cut, and he looks really, really good.

I look at Lilli and try to catch her eye, but she's seeing stars. My mind screams at her that we have a mayday situation here, but clearly, we haven't unlocked telepathy. I can't blame her, though—she's overstimulated from the pizzazz of the day and all the people we've met.

Eric Stone. The man popped up into my life for a whirlwind week five years ago, and now, here he is again, right as I'm on the precipice of one of the biggest things to ever happen to me.

"Here he is," Ash says, clapping a hand on Eric's shoulder. "This is Eric. He'll be the other bodyguard assigned to your party. Connie, he'll be your security. Lilli, I'll be yours."

Lilli looks at me with that look of "*oh shit, do you see this?*" Yeah, Lilli. I just tried having this mental conversation with you. Out loud, though, Lilli says, "Hi there."

Eric holds out a hand to shake. He's given no indication that he knows who we are, but he couldn't have forgotten, could he?

Wait, did he forget?

I take his hand and shake it. The sensation is electric, and I feel it throughout my entire body. His brown eyes are kind and a little sad—he has to remember.

Lilli, always the type to face things head-on, extends her hand. How long had Eric and I been standing there hand in hand? Time feels fake.

"You look really familiar," she says before she looks over at me. I can't say what my face is doing, but she doesn't press. "Connie, can you help me find my phone charger?"

We retreat to the bus and close the door behind us.

"What the fuck?" I say.

"Oh my God."

"How?" I sit on the couch and put my head in my hands.

"What are the odds," she muses. "What if… hmm."

"Uh oh, what dots are you connecting into a line over there?" Lilli gives me a sly smile. "Actually, I don't want to know."

"I think you do." I wave a hand in front of me, an invitation to get it over with. "I think this is your second chance!"

"No."

"Hear me out," she pleads.

I snort. "I don't have to hear you out when whatever you're about to say is certifiably insane."

"You literally wrote a song about how you wished you could have another shot together. 'Picture It' is a great song."

I shake my head. "Just because it's a great song and I wrote it doesn't mean I still feel that way. If that were true, we never would've written any other song." I don't know why I'm arguing with her; she's right about this maybe being a second chance. Thinking something to myself is different from sharing it with my best friend when we're all about to be in a tour bus together for the next three weeks.

It feels like summer camp all over again, hoping we could sit next to our crushes at the campfire and gushing about them in the cabins after lights out.

"So you're okay with him being here and being your *personal* bodyguard?" she asks.

"Sure, why wouldn't I be?"

She looks at me like I'm suffering from a concussion. "Do you really need me to answer that?"

"No." I pull my legs up and cross them on the couch. "It's fine. We weren't even dating."

"Okay, sure, but are you sure you're not just doing that thing where you minimize the seriousness of something to be more accommodating?"

I snort my derision again. "I don't do that."

"Your appendix literally had burst, and you were in so much pain that you couldn't drive, but you would've gone to work if I didn't take you to urgent care instead."

"Yes, you saved my life, I'm aware." I roll my eyes. "How was I supposed to know it wasn't just my ovaries or something?"

"Connie."

"I'm not minimizing this, Lilli. It's going to be fine. We can talk about it more later, but right now I need a break from human interaction."

She narrows her eyes, her bullshit detector measuring me. I'm not lying, though—I feel exhausted and I need to recharge. She seems satisfied and shrugs, putting her headphones on to listen to a podcast. She's such a podcast junkie. I used to be too, but Lilli started describing everything she learned to me, so I stopped listening to podcasts to spare myself from hearing the information twice. I turned instead toward audiobooks—mostly fantasy and nonfiction. Eric was the one who put me on to fantasy, actually. I restart the audiobook for *The Hobbit*.

A little while later, Eric and Ash have joined us on the bus. "We're going to take off, ladies," Ash says. "Buckle up."

There are seatbelts at the table and on the couch, but Lilli opts for the table, so I join her there. Ash is driving, Eric in the front passenger seat, and I sit with my back to him.

I close my eyes and pray these travel days go by quickly. I can't help but look back over my shoulder at him. He's talking with Ash and laughing, but I can't hear what they're saying over the audiobook. I look ahead again and see Lilli's gleeful face as I roll my eyes at her.

"Okay sure," she mouths.

What kind of cosmic joke is this?

19

5 – Connie – Then

I honestly couldn't remember the set. It's like I was in such a flow, completely lost in the music and the songs I was singing. I was mildly aware of the crowd jamming out with us, of Lilli and I bowing as they roared for an encore.

We were on cloud nine as we exited the stage and returned to the lobby to gather our guitar cases. There, another staff member told us we were free to explore the other presentations and exhibits.

"Results will be posted on the door between 5 and 7 P.M.," he said with a genuine smile. "Anyone who makes it to the final performance will receive their feedback after the show with the judges. Everyone else will get their score sheets tonight."

We thanked him and went to check in to our hotel room. After we checked in, took our luggage to the room, and changed clothes, we decided to wander around the festival. There were art displays, theatre scenes, and short films—today was all about performances.

"I kind of want to see the films," I said. "I want to just sit and relax."

The short films were being presented in an auditorium at the university campus, and when we arrived, there were some people complaining about how using a projector wouldn't be the best way to show the use of color and editing. A staff member looked panicked as she explained that those decisions were above her pay grade.

We sat in the front left as they argued. "I wish we had popcorn," Lilli said. "I'm hungry." I pulled out a bag of dried apple chips from my bag. "Oh my God, you're a lifesaver," Lilli said.

"Trust me, it's self-preservation. You're a pain when your blood sugar is low."

She nudged me playfully as the lights dimmed. An older gentleman came on stage framed in a spotlight, followed by about ten young adults.

"Thank you all for being here for the presentation of the second group of the short film category," he announced. His voice resonated through the building, his ease of projection making me think of an actor playing a general or something. "We have ten fine films to show you today. The directors are up here with me, and they will stand at the end of their film for the judges so you can see their badge numbers. Reminder to please silence your cell phones. If you need to leave at any time, we ask that you wait until the short film ends. Without further ado, let us begin!"

We started clapping as the lights went dark and the first short film began. It was horror-esque, about a girl being haunted by her boyfriend's ghost, only to find out that she was the ghost all along. The second was a found footage-style video about finding an ancient scroll, full of action and adventure.

One was really introspective about working as an online sex worker and the life of the creator when the camera was turned off. Another was a twist on *The Wizard of Oz*, where Dorothy brings her Aunt and Uncle to Oz trying to save them from poverty.

"I liked that one," Lili said as it ended.

"Me too, but I liked the sex worker one a lot too."

She nodded. "I was surprised the Wizard one was directed by a guy. It was very 'pro-matriarchy'."

"He was cute," I said, staring at the director on stage as he sat, clearly more relaxed than the others.

The speaker returned to the stage and dismissed the directors and thanked the audience and judges as I watched the cute guy walk off stage.

"I'm gonna talk to him, see if we're in any workshops together," I told Lilli.

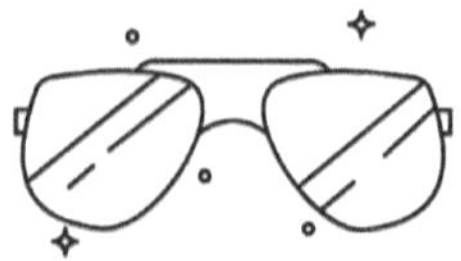

6 – Eric – Then

Bars had never really been my scene. I used to frequent gay bars with my ex-boyfriend, or I would go to sports bars with my brother and his friends where they'd all drink and yell, but I never really had a good time either way. It wasn't that I didn't drink—I just didn't overindulge. I didn't like the feeling of control slipping away, and after all the ways my friends had embarrassed themselves, I was good. *Someone* had to keep a level head.

Tonight, a bunch of the artists had wanted to hit the local spots before the tourists arrived, which was why we had been at the Lemon Drop, a hole-in-the-wall gay bar, for two hours already. I was with one of the actors in my short film, Frankie, who had played The Wizard. I didn't really want to direct—I wanted to write, but our Dorothy, Christina, had an idea and wanted me to help her write it. Directing just kind of happened because we had to hurry and get it done.

Frankie was on a date with a friend of my ex, Zach. He was a few drinks in and was already spewing his bullshit.

"Eric, it's seriously exhausting being around you. You're never any fun at bars," he taunted.

"I don't really like bars," I told him, although he already knew that.

"I think you're just not comfortable at gay bars. I think you have internalized homophobia."

I rolled my eyes. Zach was a real piece of shit. I looked over at Frankie with puppy eyes for an assist.

"You *are* kind of a downer," Frankie agreed.

This guy.

"And you've always been this way, even with Howie," Zach continued. "By the way, you should call him and apologize. Dumping him was kind of fucked up."

"I wasn't the one being fucked up," I said quietly. "You would be mad too if someone discredited you."

Frankie looked at Zach. "Wait, what happened?" Gossip queens that they were, Zach turned his whole body to Frankie in preparation.

"Eric dumped Howie like two weeks ago because of the whole bisexual thing."

"What whole bisexual thing?" Frankie asked.

I gave him a look. "Yeah, what exactly do you mean by that, Zach?"

"Now, don't get defensive, Eric." Zach took a sip from his drink. "You're a guy, you were dating a guy. That makes you gay."

"Except I'm not gay. I'm bisexual." My voice was clear, and I tried not to sound defensive, but I was so tired of this conversation.

"Gay isn't a bad word," Frankie said. "A lot of people use it as an umbrella. Besides, everyone knows bisexuality is just a way to soft launch out of the closet."

My blood didn't boil with rage—it curdled with absolute disgust. I was done. I wanted to leave. There are so many issues within the queer community, and biphobia was one of them. There were so many bisexual people on the planet, and there were still those who believed it was a phase or a stunt. As if sexuality was black and white.

"I just think you were too hard on Howie," Frankie continued, oblivious to my reaction. "I mean, look at it from his perspective."

"How about you look at it from mine? How would you feel if your partner continually attacked you for your sexuality, something you couldn't control? Imagine if it was reversed. Imagine if I kept saying, 'Howie, you're not gay, you're bi with a preference for men.' You wouldn't even be talking to me right now because it's rude as fuck."

Frankie scoffed. "That is not the same thing and you know it. He just wanted you to be proud to be with him."

"I was!"

"Then why not just say you're gay?" Frankie asked, as if it was an easy solution.

"Fucking hell, I cannot keep having this conversation." I downed the rest of my drink. "Howie's biphobia was a constant third party in our relationship."

"Biphobia?" a woman's voice behind me said. "In this political climate? Ew."

I turned to find a beautiful woman in a cropped Florence and the Machine shirt. Her dark blonde hair was in a simple braid over her shoulder, and she had glitter on her eyes the colors of the bisexual flag. Still, I didn't want to assume.

"Sorry to barge in on a very heated argument. I wasn't eavesdropping—you guys are just loud as hell."

"Here we go," Zach mock-whispered. "Another wannabe." The mystery woman narrowed her eyes.

"You're just as bad as every basic ass straight guy who hears a girl is bi and immediately assumes we want threesomes. Two girls, one dick: a straight guy's fantasy." When Zach sneered, she continued. "Bisexuality is not indicative of polyamory, and that's even its own thing that shouldn't be reduced to threesomes."

I could sense she was coming to my aid there, so I threw out a line. "Yeah," I agreed, and I felt the connection between us take hold, like drawn to like. "My ex used to make really offensive quips about how it wouldn't be considered cheating if I slept with a woman outside our relationship. He would say I wasn't bi if I was only sleeping with him, but then he'd tell everyone how he expected me to leave him for a woman."

"Damn, I didn't know he did all that," Frankie said. Zach rolled his eyes in denial and left the table to get something from the bar, and Frankie followed him with an apologetic shrug in my direction.

"One day, the queer community will be as accepting as they pretend to be," the mystery girl said. She looked at my eyes and gave me a soft smile. "You could use better companions for the rest of the night. Want to come with us?" She gestured behind her at another woman with a shirt that read, "Live. Laugh. Lesbian."

I didn't know what made me say yes. I didn't know this person, these people. I could have just as easily declined and gone home. It was one of those sliding doors moments, a life-changing decision. I could see it in front of me like an options menu in a video game. I didn't know her yet, but I wanted to.

We left the Lemon Drop and walked out into the warm Arizona night air.

"I'm Constance." She held out her hand to shake mine. "I go by Connie, though."

"Eric," I said. "Are you here for Arts Fest?"

"Yeah, we're a band." She gestured over to her friend. "This is Lilli."

"Howdy," Lilli said. *Ironically?* "You directed the Wizard of Oz one, didn't you?"

"I did!" I say, surprised. "Wait, you guys saw it?"

"Guilty," Connie said with a blush. "I noticed you when we walked into the bar, so we got the table close to you. I meant to say hi, but then I heard the biphobic shit."

"Well, whatever the catalyst was, I'm glad we're talking now." I smile at her, and I see Lilli roll her eyes, albeit playfully.

For a second, I wonder if Connie and Lilli are romantically involved and they're either laughing at me or unaware that I was flirting.

"Eric, I have a question," Lilli said. "Dorothy, is she gay? She had the lesbian walk, and I'd like to shoot my shot."

That answered my question. "She's very into women, I'll introduce you."

"Fantastic. She's hot as hell."

7 – Connie – Now

Damn him. Why does it even matter? Our history is just that – past, over, done. He really had a glow-up in the last few years; how could my memory have done him such injustice? It's like my mind put a filter on his image, the opposite of rose-colored glasses.

Most of the time, Eric keeps Ash company in the front seat—except for right now, of course. Lilli asked to sit up front so she could see everything.

This is the second time she's done this, so I find myself in my bunk bed, literally hiding from Eric under the guise of a nap. I've got my headphones, and I'm listening to Jennifer Lux's debut album, *Cavewoman*.

One of my favorite things about Jennifer Lux's music is her lyrics. I've always been more of a lyrical songwriter than a musician. I write music, of course, but it's always lyrics first with a vague melody. That's one reason why working with Lilli is so easy: she's great at layering musical compositions. I'm grateful we can still create some really fantastic songs together, even though I sometimes miss singing them.

She's a real star, though, there's no denying that, and I can say it without an ounce of bitterness or resentment, because I know she would love to have me perform again.

It's my choice to stay off stage. It's a decision I made, and she has stopped asking me to change my mind. I haven't been on stage in years. Can a person forget how to sing? There's a difference between singing in your car or with friends and performing singing. A voice is an instrument, and singing is a skill that takes practice, not a talent you're born with, although I suppose it could be both. Singing requires work, taking time to strengthen muscles through regular exercise. I haven't been doing that.

My mind continues to wander as I listen to Jennifer Lux. I don't know how exactly I ended up as a personal assistant on the payroll. It's not a big deal, I love being able to help my friend and I'm so excited to hang out with her on this tour. I just wish I felt happier. I want it to be enough. I still feel like I wasted so much time. There are moments when I think of going back out there, feeling the stage lights and being heard.

Until I remember how I don't measure up to others or even my own expectation of ability. Maybe some dreams should stay dreams. Maybe some things you think you want should be put in a box and forgotten. Maybe, if I can get myself to forget, I can be happy.

That would be a lot easier if Eric wasn't here, though, reminding me of just another thing I failed to be good enough for.

I tell myself that even if I'm not on stage singing the songs, I'm still writing them. People are still out there listening to my music. I'm still there, living the dream, just adjacent to what I thought. The bottom side of the lucky penny that no one can see.

The bus stops, and I take out my headphones and stretch. As I leave the sleeping area, I literally bump into Eric as he's coming out of the bathroom.

"Oh, excuse me," I say.

"Sorry," he says at the same time, and time freezes as we look at each other. This is the closest we've been this whole two-day drive, the closest we've been since years ago when we didn't say goodbye. I want to memorize him: his puppy dog eyes, his stubble, the little healed scar on his right cheekbone that wasn't there before.

"Alright, everyone," Ash announces. "I'm going to check us in. Then, Eric and I will escort your luggage and then you to your rooms."

When Ash closes the door behind him, Eric reminds Lilli and me to pack up anything we want in the hotel with us. I don't verbally acknowledge him, but I grab my bags. I packed according to plane rules – a carry-on, a checked bag, a personal item. I thought the structure would help me pack responsibly. When I suggested this to Lilli – since all her performance clothes would be kept separate in her dressing rooms – she laughed. She has three suitcases, one for each week. Allegedly, this is to keep her organized. I love the girl, I do. I just think this is silly.

Ash returns with the key cards, and he and Eric load up our bags on one of those bellhop carts. He's gone again, and I'm scrolling through social media, Lilli and I sending each other memes and silly videos even though we're both sitting on the same couch.

"So, you'll each have your own rooms," Ash explains in what he calls a 'safety brief'. "Lilli and Connie, your rooms are across the hall from each other. Each of your rooms will have a connecting door to our rooms. Lilli, you'll be next door to me, and Connie, you'll be next to Eric."

Ash goes on explaining that the connecting doors are for emergencies and we have the power to keep them locked, that we are under no obligation to have them unlocked, et cetera. All I can think about is how, in another life, I would have been giddy at my luck to share a hotel room with Eric. Now, it feels like the universe is taunting me just to be mean.

I kind of want to sleep in Lilli's room just to avoid the whole situation, but that seems wasteful, since Ripple Records might be extending a contract to Lilli. I don't want to make her seem frivolous.

Eric's body language is screaming that he's uncomfortable. His back is straight, his arms crossed in front of him. I know Eric—at least, I knew him—and he only stands like this when he's stressed out. When Eric is comfortable, he leans against walls or counters or whatever is in his vicinity. When he's comfortable, he puts his weight in one foot.

This stance, it's like he's trying to make himself a wall, like he's either trying to keep something out or keep something in, like when I first talked to him in the Lemon Drop. I don't know why, but this is what prompts me to finally speak to him.

"It's not a big deal."

His eyes snap to mine, and they've adopted a knife-like quality; sharp, hard, steely. "Of course not." His curt reply is aptly cutting.

Great. Somehow, I've made things worse. It's weirder now that I've broken my unofficial oath of silence, and I swallow the lump in my throat that always accompanies that old, alienated feeling. My mind starts to run, telling me that Eric hates me, that I'm dead weight on the train of Lilli's gown as she tries to fly into her career, that I am a waste of Ripple Records' resources, and that I'm a logistical nightmare for Ash.

My journal is in the bag Ash had taken to the room. While the three of us wait for him to return, I take out my phone and start typing my racing intrusive thoughts. The catharsis isn't there, and the thought of finding something small and sharp enters my mind, but I push it away. It's easier to ignore those urges now that I've been clean from self-harm for nearly six years.

I see a text from Lilli.

L: You okay?

C: Yeah, I'm fine.

Lilli gives me a look over her phone and I continue typing.

C: I guess he hates me.

L: Boys are dumb and gross.

We make it up to our rooms, and the level of security feels silly. Maybe it was just that my expectations were blown out of proportion, but from the precautions taken, I thought there would be swarms of paparazzi in the lobby and parking lot, the kind Jennifer Lux experiences.

Our rooms are on the fourth floor out of twelve floors. "Why this floor?" I ask Ash. I'm not going to be the first one to break the silence between me and Eric again.

"I like to keep it random," he replies. Ash pulls a little cloth drawstring bag out of his pocket, and into his hand pours a set of different-sized dice. I don't mean a set of cubes. No, these dice are different shapes—one is a normal six-sided die, one is a pyramid.

"Dude, you still have those?" Eric says. I look at him before I think that I shouldn't, and he's got a big smile spread across his face.

"Yeah, man, they're my lucky dice."

Lilli speaks up for me, "Wait do you guys know each other? Like, before this?"

"Yeah, we were neighbors growing up," Ash says, pocketing his bag of dice as the elevator doors open.

"I'm so tired," Lilli says as we make our way down the patterned carpet hallway. "I am so excited to sleep in a big bed." Well, there goes my idea of asking her if she wanted to hang out tonight.

"Here's your room, Lilli." Ash opens the door for her.

"Good night!" Lilli and Ash leave us, and I hear Ash locking the door from the inside. They bid each other goodnight, and I can hear them close the connecting door as the light in Ash's room turns on from under his door.

I turn, and Eric is holding my door open for me. My knees feel like bones and jelly. "He's already cleared the rooms," Eric explains, but I don't move. "Come on, Stardust, get out of the hallway."

"Don't call me that," I snap.

His eyes darken, and his voice lowers. "Do you try to be difficult, or does it come naturally?"

He sounds irritated, tired, and… sexy. Damn it. I walk in.

Eric closes the door and locks the deadbolt, the chain lock, and the handle lock. The connecting door is wide open, and I can see his nondescript black duffle bag on the bed. Does he still sleep in just his boxer briefs when he's alone, or will he wear pajamas like he did on the bus? How much has changed in five years?

He walks briskly past me into his room. As he crosses the threshold, it's like he's finally allowing himself to breathe.

"You have locks on this door as well," he says. "I'll keep mine unlocked in case you need anything."

I remind myself forcefully not to read too much into that. "Fine," I say, and neither of us move for a moment. Can he feel this tension begging for a spark? He opens his mouth to speak, and I feel my chest flutter.

"Good night, Stardust."

He closes his door, and I barely breathe, listening to hear if he changes his mind and clicks the lock. I hear him walk away from the door, and I exhale.

While I shower, I imagine my hands are his as soap bubbles glide down my body in little streams and rivers. I imagine it's his hands in my hair, and not for the first time, I regret that we never took things to the next level when we had the chance. His tenderness, his care... I know he'd satisfy every need. My traitorous brain wonders if he's awake. I quickly turn off the water, trying to block out the flow of sensual thoughts. The bathroom mirror is fogged up, and the steam permeates into the room.

Did my shower steam creep under his door? Did he think of me in the shower? I hope he did. I hope he falls asleep hoping I knock on that door.

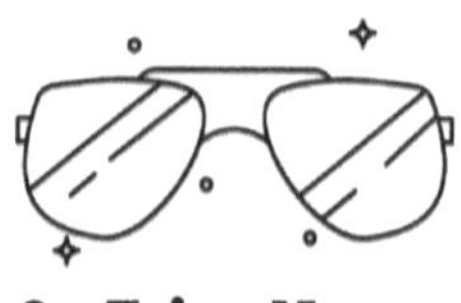

8 – Eric – Now

I wish I could say I had better things to do than listen to Connie sing in her room next to mine. It's kind of astonishing how thin these walls are. I heard her shower last night, the smell of her strawberry shampoo wafting in through the cracks around my door.

I've been up for a few hours, thanks to the wake-up call I had scheduled with the front desk. We had made good time traveling here—we're a whole day early, which means a lot of just waiting around. Connie is singing in her room, and I'm entranced. She sounds amazing, but she's being quiet. I can't hear the words, only a soft melody.

I was honestly shocked to find out that it was just Lilli, or "Lillian", as she goes by on stage, opening for Jennifer Lux. I don't know why Connie isn't singing with her, and I don't think I should ask. I tried to look up Scarlet Sofa on my phone to see if I could find out what happened between them, but of course, my feed was oversaturated with furniture. Lilli had rebranded everything on her social media accounts, but scrolling back far enough, I saw pictures of them singing together.

Connie has songwriter credit on most of Lilli's songs. From what I could tell, Connie seemed content, and there obviously wasn't any bad blood between them. So how did Connie go from a singer to a singer's assistant?

Abruptly, the music stops next door, and I go out to the hallway to see Connie opening her door. She is surprised to see me, and she quickly gives me a glare.

"What?"

"Good morning to you too, Stardust." She scowls at me, and I love how much I bother her with one word.

"I don't need an escort to go across the hall, do I?" she asks. Sure enough, Lilli opens her door to welcome Connie.

"No, ma'am," I agree. I shoot Ash a text, and he comes out. "We'll be out here."

Connie rolls her eyes as Lilli laughs. When the door is closed, Ash pulls out a fidget spinner. "Ready to tell me what's going on with you two?"

"It's ancient history," I deflect.

"That's a load of horse shit."

I pull out my phone and scroll through my photos. I find the one I'm looking for before I hand it to him.

"Holy shit, what is this?"

The photo is from when Connie and I first met, taken by Lilli outside the Lemon Drop. The flash is bright on us in the dark, and she's smiling at me while I look right at the camera. Her bi-pride glitter, my maroon shirt, and the reflection of the flash in the window behind us are the things I always look at first with this picture.

"That was when Connie and I met at the Arts Festival."

"When was this?"

"You were deployed in Japan, dealing with a lot of other stuff with your brother's divorce. Besides, Arts Fest was only a week. It's not like we were dating or anything."

"Sure, but it's obvious. Like, she's the kind of girl who has been kind to everyone she's interacted with, and then there's you. Day one, and she was shutting you out like you committed a war crime or something."

I shrug. "It's not like that. Nothing happened between us."

"Nothing?"

"Not like that. It was a really intense week, you know?"

Ash shakes his head and laughs at me. "You creative types are so funny about that. You've always been like this, citing your emotions make you more emotional, like you get to writing, and suddenly, all logic leaves your brain.

"Meanwhile, you've got this girl you're head over heels for, and you have three weeks to try and shoot your shot, but you just let her ice you out." Ash gives me a playfully sinister grin. "You should totally take the opportunity."

"She's not a prize or some conquest, Ash."

"Eric, everything is a conquest."

I roll my eyes. "Gross."

"I just mean that you have to make tactical moves."

"I don't want to just get laid. She's too special for that."

"So you don't want to sleep with her?"

"That's not what – I can't, no. I won't use her like that."

Ash strokes his beard in contemplation. "So you won't mind if I try and share her bed after Lilli is done with this leg of the tour?"

I glare at him. Ash has always been a bigger guy than me, and even though I've been hitting the gym, he could probably still knock me on my ass.

"See that look in your eye?" He laughs again. "You're ready to fight me over one comment; you are long gone. You've got feelings for her, and you should do something about it."

I shake my head. "I wasn't the one who ended things."

Ash cocks his head, and I am about to explain more when Lilli's hotel door opens, Connie and Lilli in the doorway.

"Connie is going to get me some things," Lilli says. "I'm going to take a nap for the show tonight."

"Sure thing," Ash says, and I feel the blood rushing to my face. How much of our conversation did they hear?

"Ash, will you go with me?" Connie has turned her shoulders toward him, subtly but clearly cutting me out of the conversation. Fuck that.

I cross my arms and give Ash a face that clearly means back off. He gets the message, and that sinister smile crawls back across his face.

"Sorry," Ash says, "I'm supposed to stay with Lilli. Eric can go with you." Ash does a small shrug, as if to show that his hands are metaphorically tied.

Connie visibly prickles as she turns to me stiffly. "Okay."

Two can play at this game. I look over her head and direct my question to Lilli. "What do you need?"

"Lilli needs cough drops, snacks, and other comfort items," Connie responds, clearly annoyed. "Do you need a full inventory, or can you let me handle it?" She's fiery, and it's refreshing to see her like this. "You know what? Never mind." She flips her hair back behind her. "I don't need you to babysit me." She looks at Lilli. "I'll be right back."

Ash and Lilli exchange a glance with raised eyebrows and pursed lips, and I immediately walk after her as soon as she starts to move.

"What?"

"I'm going with you, Stardust."

Connie looks over at Ash. "You guys really can't switch?"

Ash shakes his head, "Nah, I'm staying out of this."

"I don't need you to follow me like a lost dog."

"It's literally his job," Lilli chimes in.

"Well…" She's at a loss for words as her eyes search mine. "That's dumb."

"Come on, Connie. The sooner we go, the sooner it's over." She gives me an inscrutable look before she shrugs and walks over to the elevator.

It's not that she's fuming—no, it's closer to a simmer. I'm doing my best not to find it hysterical.

"How did I manage to get stuck with you?" She's asking herself, but I answer anyway, just to be a nuisance.

"Just lucky, I guess."

She scoffs, but there's no bite to her. I don't know how I can recognize her performing even now.

"The real question is how did you manage to get stuck doing midday snack runs?"

"It must be my strong foraging skills passed down for generations," she says in a sarcastic, dry, humorless tone, but there's that little dimple on her face that tells me she's playing. "Or, perhaps it's my job on payroll as Lillian's personal assistant, or my official title as best friend."

We make our way outside, and silence engulfs us as we stand waiting for a traffic light to change and let us cross the street. The sun is setting as the dinner traffic zooms about, and I feel her looking at me, but I fight the urge to meet her gaze. I keep my eyes trained on the little red LED hand, willing it to flick off and turn on the white walking stick figure. In my peripheral, I see the slight shake of her head, her hair swaying, her strawberry shampoo lifting toward me on the air as she shifts her weight. Part of me wonders just how I could be so in tune to her movements after only two days, but another part of me hates it.

The light turns to "walk", and Connie – reckless, trusting Connie – steps forward into the intersection.

I move faster than my brain could process words. There's an old white Ford F350 speeding around the corner, ignoring pedestrians, and I pull Connie into me and out of the way. I want to grab her face and check on her, make sure she was okay.

Instead, I ask, "Can't you at least look both ways before crossing the fucking street?" Adrenaline courses through my veins, coupled with the fast-crashing fear that she could have been hurt, which makes the words come out in a snarl. She flinches, and I take a deep breath to try and calm down. Her eyes are wide, her mouth hung open in shock as she realizes what had almost happened.

"The light turned, and I thought, I…" She's struggling for words when her eyes land on my hand still holding her arm. I let go, realizing I may have been holding on too tight when she starts massaging her elbow.

Yep, definitely too tight.

"Just because you're a lawful good doesn't mean you can just trust that everyone follows the rules. Most people can't read your mind either. You have to be careful. You can't trust people."

Evidently, this is the wrong thing to say, because Connie's eyes go sharp. "I know plenty about not being able to trust people, including what I've learned from you."

She turns back toward the crosswalk and makes a big show of looking left and right before walking across.

"Shit," I say following after her.

In a little convenience store with ridiculously overpriced mini travel essentials, I stay back as Connie goes right to the snack aisles.

I'm looking at a little stained glass suncatcher meant to hang from a car's rearview mirror as Connie makes her way back over to me, her arms filled.

"Eric," she says, like she's about to ask for help. Neither of us see her belt loop snag on a hook of the spinning metal display case until the entire thing crashes to the floor, tchotchkes scattering everywhere.

"Oh shit," she says as the cashier sighs at their own misfortune of being on this shift. "Sorry," Connie tells her. "I'll clean it up." I can't help but laugh at her. "Not a word." She glares at me as I help her rehang the fallen keychains.

"I had one of these once," I say. The words slip out, and I almost convince myself that I said them in my head and not out loud, except for the fact that Connie hesitates. She finds one in purple and green that has my name on it, and her fingers trace slowly along the stitching of her keychain victim.

"That was a long time ago, though," she says as she pulls herself out of the memory she's reliving. I wonder what her mind has done to that moment. How does she see it in the rearview? With rose colored glasses? Has it been preserved in honey, or worn by time and weather?

9 – Connie – Now

It's quiet most of the way back to the hotel. We're on a bridge over a river, the sun decidedly set behind the horizon, and in the dimming sunlight, I feel that magic spark. The transition from day to night, it's like its own secret space. Untouchable.

I see the crosswalk, and I feel heat invade my cheeks. I didn't need more reasons to be embarrassed in front of Eric, and then I had to go make a fool of myself in the store.

"You could talk, you know," I say, emboldened. There's so much I want to ask him, but I don't want to be vulnerable first. Not this time.

"I talk plenty," he counters. "You're the one who has been icing me out."

"I should have just had Ash come with me. I'd really rather not deal with this bullshit. I remember you, Eric. I remember you being open and communicative, at least in person."

Eric shakes his head. He's carrying the bags. Chivalrous, but he said it was because I'd likely trip and drop them, and then we'd have to go back to the store and buy more.

"Just because you have some regrets about the past…" Eric starts.

"You think you're something to regret?" I interrupt him, but he ignores me.

"That's no reason to get flattened by an F-350. I swear, Connie, there are other ways to deal with me."

I am flabbergasted. Flustered. Utterly fucked in the head. We're stopped at the crosswalk again, and I almost want to run across the street randomly (but safely) just to get back at him. Almost.

"Not everything is about you, Eric."

"Isn't it, though, Stardust?" He leans over me, a genuine smile playing with wickedness as my heart speeds up, his eyes half closed. Is he about to kiss me? He's so close, our chests almost touching.

A car skids to a stop, and I whip my head forward. The light indicates that it's our turn to cross, and I hastily make my way across, Eric by my side.

I don't know what that was, but the sooner we're separated by a wall, the better. I need to clear my head.

"I guess you're right," he says.

I smirk. "I usually am. Just ask Lilli."

"Ash could have walked you."

I make a face at him. "I'm not a dog."

He laughs, throwing his head back, and I hate how it makes my stomach flutter. "Ash could have *accompanied* you, then." I shrug; his edit is satisfactory. "But if he had, I would have missed out on you making a mess out of the keychains."

"You're insufferable," I groan, but part of me is glad there's space in all our tension and pent-up unspoken words for this lightness.

"You're adorable," he says. Unlike in the store, this was clear and loud. I stop and look at him—he's smiling at me, and it's genuine, without wicked mockery or playful teasing. He stands confidently and nudges his head toward the hotel.

I don't know how to process anything with this man.

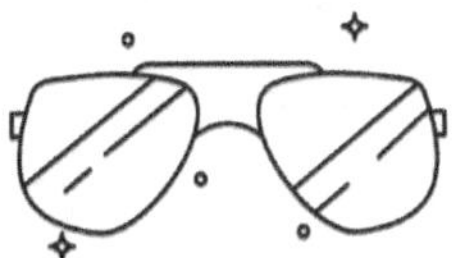

10 – Eric – Then

We had stayed up so late talking. After we left Lemon Drop, we grabbed some fast food and ate in the hotel lobby. Connie, Lilli, and I connected great. I hope Lilli didn't feel like a third wheel, although I remember it that way. Connie and I were bonding, and Lilli was there too, as bad as that is to say. She had mostly spiraled into a deep dive of social media stalking, trying to learn more about Chris. After a bit, Lilli excused herself and went upstairs to watch her vlogs.

Only after the hotel staff changed shifts did I realize I should probably head home and get some rest. Still, we talked on the phone until I parked in the driveway. Connie texted me that Lilli was snoring when she got to her room. I offered her my sympathies, but gracious Connie simply replied that Lilli couldn't help it.

We said goodnight, and I laid awake in bed as I attempted to organize all the information on Connie.

She was something else. My head was in a whirl, like I was in the twister that lifted Dorothy's house off the ground and into Oz. My dreams were in technicolor.

She had brought something out in me. I was open with her and transparent, something I had locked away.

In the morning, I don't wait to see if Connie texted me first—I called her while I got dressed. "Good morning," I say.

"Hi, good morning." Her voice was still waking up, and it sounded breathy and soft.

"You sound sleepy."

"Yeah, this guy kept me up all night, talking and talking," she teased. I could imagine her soft smile, her eyes closed.

"Hmm, someone should tell that guy to calm down," I reply.

"Nah," she laughs. "He's pretty cute."

I didn't know how to respond to that. Thankfully, though, I didn't have to, as I heard Lilli's muffled voice in the background.

"Lilli wants to know if we can go on a double date tonight and maybe go see a play?"

That almost made me pause. I knew Connie and I hit it off last night, but we just met. Are we dating? Does she want to be dating?

"That's a bit presumptuous, isn't it? They haven't even met yet," I said.

Connie's response was laced with playful annoyance directed at Lilli. "I know, but she said they started messaging last night."

"Good for them. Chris can be really cool," I told her, which is true. Chris is cool. Like, the definition of the cool kid. She's intimidating to me sometimes, but she's fun, not mean. Just that general "cool girl" vibe.

My phone dinged: a text from Chris. "Speak of the devil," I said.

"Oh?" Connie asked.

"Chris just texted me and asked if I wanted to carpool. Which would be fine, except her house is on the other side of where I am."

Lilli's mumbling in the background continued.

"I guess Chris is inviting us all over to her place?" Connie said like a question.

I met the girls outside the hotel in the valet parking area, and Lilli sat in the back while Connie rode shot gun.

"Please tell Eric what you just told me," Connie said, resting her hand briefly on my bicep. I felt the loss of her touch as soon as she pulled away.

"I told her she was great in *The Way Out*," Lilli spilled, like she could talk about this for hours and yet couldn't get it all out fast enough. "And then she sent me some of her favorite clips of me singing from my social media page, and now we're going to hang out."

"So, you both stalked each other online?"

"That's what I said!" Connie laughed, and in the rearview, I noticed Lilli blush. "You guys are practically made for each other."

I didn't know about that necessarily. A person online and over text could be so different than the person in real life. I might have agreed if they had met in person first, but I didn't know.

"Damn, she's hot," Connie said as Lilli showed her a picture. "But this is so staged."

"She said she just woke up," Lilli argued.

"But who sleeps in a sports bra and gold chain necklace? That sounds uncomfortable."

Lilli ignored Connie and showed me the phone, and I glanced at it as we stopped at a red light.

"Yeah, that's Chris," I confirmed.

"She's so butch!" Lilli exclaimed. "She was so femme in the short film. Get you a woman who can do both." Then, she poked at Connie. "Or don't. You leave this one to me and hang out with your boy."

Connie's blush was so adorable, I wanted to put my hand against her cheek to feel the warmth. I was so excited to spend more time with her.

We arrived at Chris' house with Lilli practically buzzing in the back seat. Chris let us in wearing a loose-fitting, white button-up shirt, actively rolling up the sleeves as she opens the door. Her black hair is styled back with some parts hanging in front in a very K-pop fashion, her black pants and signature gold chain on.

"Hey." Her husky voice was casual, in a cool-girl-chic type of way. Lilli was in cool girl mode too, but I saw her fangirling in the car. "Come on in."

"Can I use your bathroom?" Lilli asked immediately.

"Sure thing. I have my own in my room. I'll show you." And just like that, Chris and Lilli disappeared as Connie and I sat on the couch in the living room.

"It seems like a big house," Connie said as we turned on a show on the TV. After the next episode started, Connie and I looked over towards the direction where Lilli and Chris went off to.

"I assume they're getting along in there," I said. Connie laughed so hard she snorted, and I realized the implication of what I said. "Not what I meant," I laughed.

"Lilli is probably asking about everything in her room. I hope Chris likes talking about herself."

"Or maybe it's Chris asking Lilli everything," I suggested.

We were quiet, trying to listen. "I can hear talking for sure," Connie said.

I lowered the volume of the television and turned on the couch to face her. "I'd like to know more about you, Connie."

She blushed again and looked down. "Oh?" Is that so hard for her to believe?

"Are you bashful or shy?" I wondered aloud.

"I'm just… flattered but also nervous."

I thought about that for a second; I was nervous too. "That's okay. I can go first. Ask me anything."

She looked over at the television, but she was thinking; I could almost see the question forming in her mind. "Ocean or space?"

"Space," I said, the answer instinctual. "The final frontier and what not."

She shook her head. "Ocean. There's so much undiscovered, so many questions, and it's right here."

"The ocean is scary and full of sea monsters, though," I countered.

"And space could be too!" She looked at me, the conversation bringing back some ease and comfort.

"There's no evidence of that. There is, however, lots of evidence of creepy things in the ocean." I felt confident in my reasoning, but Connie just shook her head.

"Exactly."

11 – Connie – Then

Eric and I spent the whole day together. After Chris's house, we went back to the festival and attended some workshops. We ate lunch with Chris and Lilli, both very cuddly in the booth across from us at the café. We discussed the art posted in the café as an exhibit, part of the festival.

Eventually, Chris and Lilli went to look at a photography exhibit and lecture on auditioning, and Eric and I ended up back in the hotel lobby, in our same chairs as the other night. It was starting to feel like our spot already. He was showing me fan made edits online, trying to convince me to rewatch the entire Lord of the Rings franchise.

"Why do you like it so much?" I asked him, not able to tell the difference between the movies in each trilogy. They were starting to blend together for me, probably because I was distracted by the childlike joy in his eyes.

"I got really into Lord of the Rings because of my dad," he confided in me. "He got sick when I was in my junior year of high school."

I wanted to reach out to him, to comfort him, but I felt like I didn't know how to react to his vulnerability.

"Besides," he said with a small smile, "Aragorn is the peak of masculinity." He wanted to alleviate the emotional heaviness and I obliged, taking the chance to spar.

"I don't know—can anyone really be compared to Orlando Bloom?"

"Aragorn is the king!" Eric parried, and I had to suppress a smile. "He is gentle, good, kind, formidable, strong, reliable, and let's be honest, the emotional maturity he has is phenomenal." He paused and looked up another video. "Although, that could be because of his elven heritage and him being the age of a grandpa with a young body."

"Ah, yes, another unrealistic expectation for men," I agreed. "You know, you're trying really hard to convince me here, Eric. Did you write some self-insert fanfiction or something?" His mouth snapped shut, and a pink flush danced across his cheekbones. "Holy shit, you did."

"I did not write self-insert fanfiction," he said, as if he was backpedaling. "There was just that one short film…"

"Oh my God." I pushed his shoulder and pointed ecstatically to his phone. "Show me, show me now. I need this."

"No, you don't." His attempt at pushing aside my focus was weak, though, and he knew I wouldn't back down. There was no containing the grin on my face as Eric signaled defeat and pulled up a video.

"I know the language is too flowery and the costumes are garbage, but I was seventeen when I made this, and it was my first film project," Eric said, apologizing for his art before letting me even consume it.

I actually thought it was pretty good.

The camera panned to an older man, his cane in one hand, a wizard staff in the other.

"That's my dad," Eric said quietly. "He refused to use a walker because he said Gandalf wouldn't. He passed not long after this."

"I'm so sorry." Even though it was an automatic reaction, I meant it. "I can't imagine."

"Thanks."

Silence filled the space between us as the video faded to white, like the air itself had become delicate.

"It's a little cringe overall," Eric said, once again easing the tension so effortlessly.

"I think it's really sweet. This is a precious thing to have." I wanted to keep all embarrassment from him so he may never feel shame with me, and part of me wanted to tell him that my heart is a home with a room ready for him to move into. I wanted to see the baby pictures and home videos, wanted him to trust me with the skeletons in his closet, wanted him to know he could bring down the shoebox filled with memories and forgotten dreams, that maybe those dreams could still come true.

I don't utter a single word of it, though. I just penned it into a new song.

12 – Connie – Now

Backstage is surreal. The fact that we are backstage at a sold-out stadium for one of the biggest tours of all time… and that my songs are going to be the opening act? Yeah, surreal is the only word for it.

It makes me think of Pinocchio inside the belly of the beast, staring at the skeletal structure of this thing that is literally and figuratively so much bigger than you. Small fish, meet big pond.

Lilli and I walked the stage before they opened the gates to the audience. Sound check went by quickly, and I watched as stagehands and crew members crawled around in their routine. Countless wires were grouped together and taped or tied along the floor and scaffolding, as intricate as tree roots or a nervous system. As Lilli tested a mic and back up mic, I was in complete awe over the sheer quantity of everything: cables, workers, lights, buttons, seats, people… and yet, it was efficient. I find myself overwhelmed, unable to focus on capturing the details. I do my best to make sure I don't look like my eyes are glazing over.

Now, we're backstage, and Lilli is about to perform.

"Go out there with me," she says, her eyes wide.

"What?" I doubt I heard her right.

"I already cleared it with Jennifer Lux and Ripple Records. I talked to Tops, and she said it was fine. Come on, Connie." Lilli takes both my hands in hers as she pleads with me, "We should be doing this together."

I don't know what brought this on. She knows I haven't performed in years. Even though I miss it, feel that old familiar pull to be in the spotlight, I resist it. If the reception from the audience was bad, it could trigger an episode.

"Lilli, I can't…"

"Sure you can! They're your songs!"

"I haven't rehearsed with you. You have dances and stuff…"

"I have a costume for you in the dressing room. Come out for the acoustic song." Lilli is waving down a crew member, who hands me a microphone. "You said you might want to perform again, so do it tonight!"

I hand her the microphone and take a step back.

"Lilli, I appreciate what you're trying to do, but I'm not ready tonight. Maybe if I had time to prepare, then maybe…"

A glint of promise in her eye, Lilli hands the microphone back to the crew. "So before the end of my time opening this tour, you're going to sing with me."

There's a thirty second clock up on the big screen, and I can see it on the monitor beside us. I decide that we need to focus on the current moment.

"Dude, this is it! You're doing this!" I hype her up because that's what best friends do. "I'm so fucking proud of you, Lilypad. Go kick some ass!" We jump up and down, getting her energy up and nerves out.

The screen says ten seconds, so I hug her tight and then run off stage in the back area where I can still see her perform.

She is immediately on for the crowd—stage presence was never an issue for her. The crowd is mostly full already, but some of the seats are still empty. That makes sense, though; people are here for Jennifer Lux. I see people heading over to the merch trucks and restrooms, but mostly people I can see are singing along with Lilli. She opened up with not the most streamed song, but the second most. I'm watching from behind the stage, but I'm thirsty, and I can't see her face anyway, so I look around for some water.

I see a flat of water bottles on the floor by a crew member with a headset on.

"Excuse me, can I have one of those?" I ask.

The crew member nods and points over toward a small tent with two tables and some chairs. "No water by the equipment, please."

There are a few people here, but I haven't met any of them, mostly band members for Jennifer's set. I recognize one of the male dancers, who has gone viral online. He's hot, and the choreography gives so much, if you know what I mean. I think about going up and saying hi, but he gets a call and leaves the tent.

Maybe later.

I start drinking my water as fast as I can so I can go back to watch Lilli's set when I see Michael, Jennifer Lux's drummer. He has this aura about him that captivates me. It's enchanting. He's lounging back on a bench with a velvet button up shirt, one arm along the top of the back of the bench, the other holding what looked like a cocktail. His hips are low on the seat, causing him to slouch, his chest open wide. It made me think of that one yoga class Lilli and I took for a few weeks, where the instructor would tell us to "face our hearts to the sun."

Michael has golden hoop earrings on, and on one side, a second earring of what looks like a feather. There is also a collection of different beaded bracelets on his wrist holding his drink. We make eye contact, and his smile spreads like butter on warm toast. He has a faint goatee, not really the same shadow as Eric.

The comparison comes without warning. I break eye contact and shake my head as I finish my water and head back to the back of the stage. Lilli has started the third song, and the crowd is with her, singing along. I see some of the band members heading up to their spots for the show.

"She sounds great," a voice purrs in my ear. Handsome and radiating trouble, Michael is behind me, sans cocktail. "I'm Michael," he says, as if I don't already know. As if I didn't make sure I knew every band member's name before we got on the bus.

That means I already know this guy. I know he oozes sexual prowess. I could have a good night with him if I wanted to.

Maybe it'll help get Eric out of my head.

"I'm Connie," I say, and I put my hands in the back pockets of my jeans to expose my breasts subtly. I see how he notices.

"Are you going to stick around and watch me play?" he asks.

"It'd be silly to miss out on a chance to see a sold-out tour," I reply. Cat and mouse games only work when there's a little chase. "We'll just have to see what happens."

Michael leans in and whispers in my ear, "I'd love if you watched. It'd give you a preview to how well I can keep tempo."

I have to give him credit for that line. I feel myself blush despite myself, but I don't balk at his forwardness. I continue the game. Men like him always want something they think they can't get easily.

"Maybe. Lillian might need me." I smirk at him, letting him know that I'm intrigued but promising nothing.

"Hmm," he says in my ear. "She could join us."

I laugh at that because maybe this guy's gaydar is broken, or maybe he legit never noticed that Lillian's branding is all colors of the lesbian pride flag. "You're not her type, sorry."

He missed the message. He taps my nose with his finger and says, "We'll see."

As he walks away, I decide that maybe I could sleep with him at some point on this tour, but I don't think I'd get much enjoyment out of it. It'd end up being a headache later if ever it came out.

I don't want it to negatively impact anything in the future. It's too risky to sleep around with other professionals, I remind myself.

Lilli is doing an amazing job, and her set is wrapping up. I wonder if I'll take her up on her offer and go out and sing a song with her at some point over the next eight shows. This is going to catapult her career to the next level, and maybe mine too. Many of these songs she's singing I either helped write or wrote in their entirety. I think briefly about those fish that latch onto whales to help them travel across great distances. Is that how I am? Attaching myself so securely to Lilli that I can ride the wave of her success into my own? No, that's not fair. I work hard at what I do. There's a reason why I get writer credit on these songs. If my best friend wants to use my words, then so be it. If she rises to fame and I happen to rise with her, what's the harm? She'll give voice to my words. It'll be fine.

So why do I have this sinking feeling that I'm dooming myself to a life in shadows?

It's not until this moment that I realize Eric is watching me. He's positioned in front of the stage on the floor, in that space between the stage and the crowd. He's got fire in his eyes that tells me he saw the flirtation with Michael, and he's seriously jealous.

Part of me feels like a kid caught with her hand in the cookie jar, and part of me feels indignant. He has no claim to jealousy.

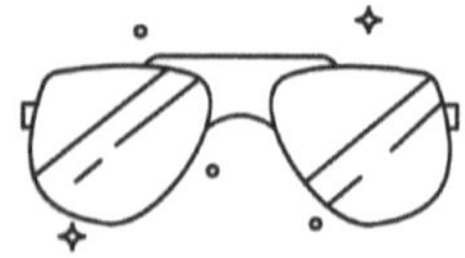

13 – Eric – Now

Something feral within me wants to claim Connie, and I check it at the door. I can't be a possessive asshole; that's not going to help anyone. Still, I can't deny the fact that watching her flirt with that guy pissed me off to new lengths. I *had* noticed that *same* guy making out behind a tour bus when we got here.

Rockstar lifestyle, I guess.

It's hard to imagine Connie would be into that, but maybe I don't know her like I thought I did. After Lilli's set, I make my way backstage and prepare to escort them to their dressing room. Lilli is quiet, probably crashing from the adrenaline of being on stage, which means Connie is quiet. She's back to avoiding my eye contact.

Lilli's dressing room is two parts: a sort of lounge area and a bathroom. She goes in the bathroom to change and wash her face, leaving Connie and I in the lounge area.

The silence is nipping at me until I can't take it.

"You should stay away from him," I say.

Her eyes snap to mine, and there's fire in them. She's angry and I get it, but come on. A sleaze is a sleaze even if he is a rockstar. Can't she see that?

"You don't get to say that," she says dismissively.

"You could get any person you want, you really want Michael Soren? That guy is a petri dish waiting to happen."

She leans forward, "What does that even mean?"

"Sure, Stardust, he's a hot rockstar, but I don't care. He's a jerk. Ash told me about him."

"And what did Ash say?"

All Ash had said was not to trust him within ten feet of our girls, but that it shouldn't be an issue, since we were going to be in our own bus. "He's just… bad news."

"You know, Eric," her irritation comes out thick, "you've got a lot of opinions about one conversation I had. I wonder where all this concern for my wellbeing have been the last five years."

It's like a slap in the face. "Phones work both ways, Connie."

"You hurt me!" She's standing now, pointing a finger at me like an accuser. "Because you didn't even try to fight for me. One week. We knew each other less than one whole week, and somehow, that was enough for you to break my heart." She shakes her head, and quietly, not looking at me, she says, "I hadn't felt that weak in a long time. I didn't realize how fragile I had become."

"Did you think I wanted to hurt you?" Her silence guts me. "Connie…" I want to hold her, to take her in my arms, but she steps back. "I wanted you to be happy. After a week in a daydream with you, I went home to find my ex-boyfriend had come back to our apartment from his vacation. We had to find new separate places to live and break our lease. I had to get a second job to pay rent, and I still couldn't swing it. I ended up moving back home, but the financial stress built up. That week with you was something out of a fairytale, but I was drowning when I had to come back to reality."

Her voice is quiet again. "It was real to me."

"Of course, it was real," I sigh. Nothing is coming out right. How can I tell this girl what she means to me and not sound insane? I feel insane.

"But clearly it didn't matter," she says, "I didn't matter. I understand, Eric. I understand that you had very important things to take care of. I understand that you had immense stress and pressure. I'd even understand if our week at the festival was just an exciting distraction for you. Because I always understand. But that does not change how it hurt me, how you hurt me, when you shut me out. How it still hurts because you gave me hope, and I thought we both respected each other enough to be honest. But even then, hell, even now, I understand why you weren't, and I hate that I can't let myself hate you for it."

She's right in my face, searching my eyes. I wonder if she can see the hurt there from back then, from letting her go, the hurt I see in hers. She's so close, and those eyes…

She's so close to me that our noses bump slightly, but neither of us turns away or steps back. She reaches up and touches my face, and it's like the invitation every molecule in me has been waiting for, because I let go, and my mouth is on hers in an instant.

It's a lustful and hungry kind of kiss, open mouthed, as if we need to devour each other in this moment. My hands are gripping her, one on her lower back and the other cupping her ass. Connie's arms have wrapped around my neck, one hand clawing up my neck and into my hair.

"Fuck," I say.

Then, there's a knock at the door.

"Can I come in?" It's Ash, speaking through the door.

Connie and I jump apart as she turns to the mirror to fix her hair. "One second!" She turns to me and pleads, "Not a word to anyone please."

I agree that I would rather *not* start the rumor mill before I even know the truth.

14 – Connie – Then

Day three of the festival, and Lilli and I woke up too late for the free breakfast provided by the hotel. Instead, we raided my snack bag for protein bars and individual bags of chips, both kind of emotionally hungover from the day before. Lilli, on the other hand, was buzzing from her time with Chris.

"She's such a gentleman," she said as she washes her face. "And her skin care routine is ridiculous. Like, that kind of dedication is hot."

"You guys really hit it off. What were you guys doing in her room?"

Lilli blushed. "Oh, you know, she was showing me her bookshelf."

"Her bookshelf?"

"Yeah, and then she read me some Shakespear. You know me—I don't really understand half of it, but she was saying really pretty words, and then we kind of made out."

I laughed. "Yeah, Eric and I assumed as much."

Shame and embarrassment rose in her, but it wasn't what I intended. "Lilli, hey, I didn't mean anything by it."

Lilli crumpled on the floor and sobbed, and it took me by surprise. "Lillipad, what's wrong? Did she hurt you?" Lilli shook her head emphatically. "Did she say something mean to you?"

Again, Lilli shook her head no, now accompanied with a big sniffle as I handed her a tissue. I was running out of guesses as to what happened.

"So, what happened? Why are you upset? Do I need to fight someone? Because, I mean, I'm not really a fighter, so I'll have to try my best."

Lilli coughs out a wet laugh. "I just…I didn't expect it to happen this way. I don't want to say I regret it, because I don't think I regret my first time being with her, but…"

"Woah, wait, you guys had sex? I thought you said you made out."

"We did make out! And then some."

"Oh my gosh, Lilli! Wait, why didn't you tell me?"

She kind of flung her arms around, gesturing at me. "Because you're you."

"What does that mean?"

"I mean, you've slept with people, and it never seemed like a big deal to you."

My mouth dropped open. "I have done you a disservice then, and I apologize. Lilli, it's always a big deal to me when I have sex with someone. I didn't talk about it too much because I knew you were a virgin and I didn't want you to be uncomfortable."

Lilli and I held eye contact for a moment before we started laughing. "I thought there was something wrong with me this whole time because I was freaking out, and I was trying to be chill!"

We eventually migrated over to her car and drove over to the university campus, where there were some musician workshops happening.

"So, how was it?" I asked.

"Well, thankfully, Chris is as much of a top as she seems. The stereotype was right this time. Butch women are tops. She's also kind of a dom, if that makes sense?"

"Kinky," I teased.

"No, literally. Like, ropes and stuff."

"Were you okay with that?" I asked, concerned my friend was pushed into something she wasn't ready for.

"Yeah, actually. I was so nervous, I kind of liked being restrained. If I couldn't move, I couldn't do something wrong."

That made me laugh so hard, I started crying, and Lilli blushed harder.

"I'm sorry, I'm not laughing at you."

"Yes, you are."

"No, I'm not! It's just not my typical M.O., if you know what I mean."

"Do you mean the ropes, or the not moving part?" Lilli asked, actually looking for clarification.

"I mean being a bottom, I guess. I like being in charge."

She nodded. "Well, that makes sense, but maybe that's just because you have more experience. You know what you like and how to ask for it."

I shrugged.

"Have you and Eric gotten physical at all?"

"No," I answered honestly. "We haven't even gone to a bedroom. We haven't kissed. I don't think either of us were looking for a hook up or anything, so it's just been nice getting to know each other. And you know I'm doing a year of abstinence. Once I'm clean from self-harm for a year, then I can open myself up to that again."

"You're close though, right? It's been almost a year."

"Two months to go."

Lilli was quiet for a moment, the only sounds the hum of the car and the blast of the air conditioner trying its best.

"I'm not trying to trigger you, so if you don't want to talk about it, just tell me to shut up." She tentatively looked over at me, and I waited for her to continue. "Why are you abstaining from sex as part of your recovery from cutting?"

I let out a breath, collecting my thoughts. I hadn't really talked to anyone about it, not even my therapist. "I mean, sex is great. I just, I had gotten into the habit of making myself feel like shit for it. I would sleep with people just so I could use it as cannon fodder against myself, which would drive me to cut again. It became part of the cycle, and I want to get back to a place where I have sex with someone because I like them and want to feel good."

"Oh, I didn't know." Lily looked at me at a loss for words. "I'm sorry I asked."

The majority of the day was spent at workshops, including a tour of a recording studio. Lily and I sat between two other people while the person in charge of the tour spoke about the different machines and sound boards. We even got to go back and try out the recording studio, just to know what it felt like.

When I stood behind that microphone, I felt the rest of the world slip away. I knew there was going to be a whole roomful of people on the other side of the glass looking at me, but it didn't matter. I felt in my bones the certainty that this was what I wanted to do for the rest of my life. I wanted to make music. I wanted to sing my songs to crowds of people who connected to the lyrics. I wanted to write songs for the people who needed a way to express themselves but didn't have the words for it. I wanted to help people articulate complicated feelings and find catharsis.

Those feelings and that instinct I had, the desire I felt, was multiplied when I checked my e-mail as I got back into Lilli's Buick.

"Holy shit," I said, slapping her lightly but repetitively on the arm. "Lilli, we made it."

In my e-mail sat an unopened message from the festival. All I could see at that point was the subject line, which read, "Congratulations, you've made it to the finals!"

I opened it and looked at the rehearsal blocks—we were set to have rehearsal that evening.

Lilli and I each texted Chris and Eric the good news, and Lilli came back with an…interesting proposal.

"Okay, Connie, I need you to have an open mind."

I put my phone down because it sounded serious,. Lilli had a look in her eye that could have either been delusion or excitement.

"What if we moved to New York next year?"

Okay, delusional. "Why would we do that? There are so many recording studios in California with the record labels we want to sign with."

"But there are also studios for the same labels in New York," Lilli said, if we were already in negotiations.

"Why would we move to New York exactly?"

Lilli spoke softly, like in a game. "Chris is going to an acting program there?" She wanted that to be a good enough reason for me, and she phrased it like a question because she knew it wouldn't be.

"Lesbians moving in together right away is just a stereotype, Lilli. You don't have to make it a reality."

"But I like her a lot."

"Did she ask you to move out there already? Do you think it's that serious?"

Lilli shrugged. "She didn't really invite me in a formal way, just kind of casually started talking about us living there together."

"Together? Me, you, and Chris?"

"Well, mostly just me and her, but I won't go without you. We're bandmates."

"I don't know," I said. How could I respond to that? I'd either be denying her happiness with a partner she seems to really like and trust, or I would be robbing myself by giving in to an arrangement I didn't want.

"Just think about it. It's months away."

15 – Connie – Now

Lilli is riding the wave of post-performance bliss, a great show leaving her inflated like a helium balloon.

"I'm so ready for sleep," she says in the silence of the car. Ash is in the passenger seat while Eric drives, Lilli and I in the back. "And a bath!" She practically moans at the thought. "I have some of that champagne you bought yesterday, Connie, and my favorite podcast uploaded a new episode. Hot girl bath is calling my name."

I nod and try to be engaged, but Eric and I make eye contact in the rearview as we pass through the beam of a streetlamp. Lilli isn't the only one riding the adrenaline of tonight's events. That kiss…it changed something in me. I want this man like I've never wanted anyone before. I think he can tell, too, because I feel the car go a little bit faster.

"Which podcast is this?" Ash asks. "We've talked about so many, it's hard to keep track." His joke flies past me, and I fail to get myself to pay attention. I'm looking out the window, praying for green lights all the way back to the hotel.

Lilli and Ash keep talking, and I think she knows something is up, because as we park, she catches my eye and gives me a questioning look and a thumbs up.

I nod, and she's clearly not convinced, but she lets it go. We climb out of the car, and it's a quiet elevator ride to our floor. The space between Eric and I is so charged, it's a miracle my hair isn't flying up from the static.

Ash and Lilli get into their rooms after brief good nights, and I turn to mine. I'm mentally preparing to open the connecting door and let Eric in from his room when, right before my door closes behind me, his hand pushes it back open.

Eric lifts me up, and I wrap my legs around his hips on instinct. His arms around me feel sure and strong. Unwavering. Through the curtain of my hair, I see the hotel door close. He breathes me in, and something about him savoring the scent of my shampoo stirs a primal ache in me. I scrape my teeth along a small portion of his neck and suck the skin into my mouth before leaving it with a kiss, and he groans in response. He wants me, but I already know that. There's a difference between knowing something and feeling it. I can feel his want now in his pause.

"Trust me?" he asks, and I hum in agreement as I feel him adjust his arms. I unwrap my legs, and they drop to the floor as his kind eyes look at me the same way they did in another time, in another place, lying on a mattress across from each other on the night I pushed him away.

Looking at me like I'm the fucking Milky Way. I wanted him then too, but this time, I don't want to wait.

I take his hand and lead him to the bed, turning so that I'm standing with my back to the bed, just in front of the little ottoman that doubles as a footboard of sorts.

"Trust me?" I ask as I grip his belt buckle. I want his consent as much as I know he wants mine.

His eyes are dark with lust as he gives me a quick nod of his head, and I immediately go to unbuckle his belt.

Unfortunately, I fumble. I don't wear belts very often, if ever, and I haven't really gotten used to having acrylic nails. Eric holds my shoulders in a very clear "wait one moment" kind of way. His hand moves down my temple, along my jaw, and his thumb flicks down my bottom lip, causing a small pout.

"Those lips," he whispers, his eyes hooded.

Then, he grabs his belt buckle with one hand and, with the opposite forearm, pulls his belt out in one fluid motion. It's fucking *hot*. With his belt discarded haphazardly on the corner of the bed, I go to work pulling down his jeans and grey boxer briefs.

Some small part of me is surprised at their normalcy, expecting something *Lord of the Rings* pattern to represent Eric's inner nerd. That would be too literary for reality, I guess.

I lower the waistband, and his already-hard cock springs up as I free it from its confinement, a small bead of precum already making itself known.

Biology be damned, though, I want some foreplay. He grabs a fist-full of my hair and pulls me in for a kiss. I kiss him back, our tongues caressing each other briefly before his grip relaxes and I pull away to sit on the ottoman and pull off his shirt.

There's a small tattoo there on his chest: "from thine eyes" in a thin, scrawling font. I tuck it away in my mind as I run my fingers down his torso, along his hips, the tops of his thighs to his knees, lightly scraping the edges of my nails along his skin. He takes a deep breath through the nose to control his shiver as I slide my hands along him, fingers fanned out through the fine dark leg hair, up his inner thigh to either side of him, but not quite touching him where he wants me, letting the anticipation build.

Without warning, I grip his cock in my right hand, his balls in my left. I'm a little nervous that I might do something wrong here—I don't know what pressure is pleasure and how much pressure is painful.

"Tell me if it hurts, okay?" I ask.

"You feel amazing, Stardust." His voice is deep, a groan on an exhalation.

I give him a coy smile and hold his gaze as I open my mouth and flatten my tongue along the underside of his dick, moving my way up to the tip. His eyes flutter shut as his body shivers, and I relish in the power trip of his pleasure. When I reach the top, I roll my tongue in a circle clockwise, then counterclockwise, around the tip. The precum is salty and smooth, and I let myself drool sloppily. More lubricant can only help.

"Fuck, Constance." His arms are flexed, and I feel like he's retraining himself. I close my lips around him and take as much in as I can; when I pull back, I suck on the tip like a straw. Back and forth, I keep my jaw relaxed as I try and take him deeper each time. I gag, but I pull him in by wrapping a hand around his thigh.

"Be careful," he says.

"Did I hurt you?" I ask as I come up for air.

"No, I just don't want to come before I can please you."

I make slow, torturous strokes while rolling my wrist like I'm rolling quarters before I take his balls in my mouth. I focus on the way his knees shake when I suck on them, and I hum a moan, only to be rewarded by Eric's "oh, God" response. I go back to a big swipe of my tongue from balls to tip and then lay a soft, sweet kiss on his inner thigh.

"Clothes. Off. Now."

I smile as I remove my crop top. Luckily for both of us, I wasn't wearing a bra. He practically tears off his shirt and pulls me to my feet so he's on his knees in front of me, pulling down my sweat shorts and underwear in one move.

"I don't know how long I'll last, so let me enjoy you for a while first."

He lifts me and sets me on the bed, and I let out a little laugh because I am so elated already. "You don't have to," I say, mainly because I'm a little self-conscious about his face being so up close and personal with an area of my body I can only see if I hold a mirror at a specific angle.

"You don't think I'm doing this for you, do you?" The darkness in his green eyes glint with mischievous playfulness. "Because you'd be mostly right, but this is for me."

His rough hands are paradoxically gentle as they press my knees down and apart before he kisses my inner thigh down, down, down. Eric settles himself at an angle, his shoulder beneath thigh, his head almost laying on me like I'm a pillow. His soft curls tickle my inner hip, and my entire body tenses slightly at the feathery feeling of his hair. His forearm is weighing down on my inner thigh like a vice, keeping me in place, as if to prevent me from obscuring his view. His thumb pulls at my skin, opening me to him a bit more.

I wonder what's going through his mind, if he's getting second thoughts. I wonder a million things as my mind races and then stutters to a halt as his mouth makes contact. His tongue mimics my performance with a wide, slow stroke up to my clit, where he sucks softly. I'm trying to focus, to memorize this reality I've fantasized a hundred times, but it all just feels so good, all I can think is *more* as the details slip through my mind like water.

"Damnit, Eric," I moan, my back arching. I'm gripping my hips because I don't know what else to do with my hands. I don't trust them; they'll coil their fingers into Eric's hair, pulling him closer as I grind against his face, but I don't want to disrupt what he's doing because it feels so good, I almost want to let my hands have their way. Almost.

"Is something wrong?" His question is playful, like he's teasing me.

"Fuck me," I order, and he eats me hungrily, like a man starved, reduced to pure, animalistic need. His mouth and hand work in harmony, and I'm mildly aware of how soaked everything beneath me has become. Electricity jolts through me in waves, and I come twice more before he pulls himself up.

"How're you doing, Stardust?" He's like a juxtaposition, checking on me and wanting validation at the same time. I give him a lazy content smile. "Do you want to stop? Or would you like me to keep going?"

I hook my hand around the back of his neck and pull him in. He hesitates, but I don't care. I taste and smell myself all over him, clinging to his stubble.

"Eric," I say as lock eyes with him, "I want you to fuck me."

"Yes, ma'am."

He rubs the length of his swollen cock along my opening, so warm compared to the cool air that had been there moments before. I grab fistfuls of the comforter as the head of his dick pushes its way into me. I'm so sensitive that I feel deliciously delirious, and I gasp as he pushes his full length into me, so much bigger than I thought he would feel.

"You feel so fucking good," I tell him, and the praise fuels his fire.

He takes my right leg and brings it across to the other side of my body so my left leg is practically straight between his knees, the rest of me in a corkscrew position. My shoulders and upper back still lay flat on the mattress, my hips twisting over to the side, and his hands pushing down on my upward hip slightly to keep me in place as he plows into me so deep, he's practically punching my cervix. It almost knocks the air out of me, and in this corkscrew position, my diaphragm is compressed, but I'm breathing fine. It's a good kind of pain.

"God, Constance," he moans, almost a plea.

"I'll be your goddess," I can't help but smile as he continues to thrust full force into me. "If this is how you'll worship me."

"I'll worship you forever," he says, and my heart flutters at the accidental confession that he could want this, want *me*, forever, "but I can't last much longer." His face is a delicious cocktail of pleasure and focus as he starts to slow.. "I'm going to come if I keep this up."

"So do it," I say. We hadn't talked about it. "I'm on the pill." It's almost instant—I feel him spill himself deep within me, the telltale, involuntary twitch of his cock as his whole body shudders and he collapses on top of me. He rolls onto his side, cradling me in his arms, the movement making him pull out of me.

"Amen," he says.

He breathes in the scent of my hair and plants little kisses along my temple before I feel him drift off to sleep as his breathing slows. My body rests, safe, as my mind starts to wander. I think about how Lilli will react when she finds out. Would Eric want to tell people?

I must have fallen asleep daydreaming, because I am startled awake when my phone rings. No, not my phone —the hotel phone, Eric's room. As the disorientation fades, Eric answers it, and I grab my clothes and make it to the bathroom. Thanks for the number one sex ed lesson, mom. By the time I come out of the bathroom fully dressed, Eric has moved on to a call on his cell phone, completely ready for his day.

"I understand. I'll be there in ten minutes." The call ends, and he walks over to me, enveloping me into a big hug. "Duty calls."

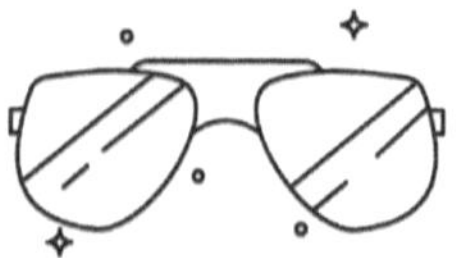

16 – Eric – Now

It's the next night when I knock on Connie's door. I haven't gotten a chance to talk to her since yesterday, since last night. What a fucking night. I have been living on a cotton candy cloud since I left her room, all too aware that the smallest bit of rain could destroy everything.

What is even happening now? Are we going to move forward? Back? We haven't talked about expectations.

Connie opens the connecting door, her hair in two braids, wearing fuzzy sweats. "Hey," she says, and immediately, I sense her walls are up, the storm rolling in towards my cotton candy cloud.

"I didn't mean to bug you," I start back pedaling.

Her eyes assess me. "You didn't. I was just about to put on an under-eye mask." She leaves the door open and turns back toward the mirror in the bathroom while I stand there awkwardly in the door. I watch as she peels small green delicate pads from a jar and places one under each eye. "Can you set a timer for fifteen minutes?"

I take out my phone and set the timer. "Can I come in?"

Her brows pinch together. "I think we should talk." She sits cross legged on the floor on her side of the door way, and I sit down too, my back against the foot of my bed and my arms crossed on my knees.

She's not kicking me out, so this is a good sign, right? Letting me in, but not in her room. The imagery is interesting for a screenplay.

"It's been a while," she smiles.

"Less than a day," I say.

Connie shakes her head. "I mean since Arizona." Her eyes drop to her hands, where she's fiddling with the drawstring of her sweats. "What have you been up to?"

"Are we about to have small talk, Stardust?"

"No, I just," Connie lets out a puff of air, "well, you're not exactly making a movie right now. How did you get… here?"

I let out a long breath. I want to be open with her too—that's how these things work, right? "I'm the provider for my family," I say with a shrug.

"Oh my God, you have a family?" She jumps up, her face turning red with rage. She grabs a pillow from her bed and is prepared to throw it at me. "You fucking pig—"

"Woah! No! I mean my mom and my sister!" My hands are up to try and catch the pillow, but she hesitates as she processes. Then, she tosses the pillow on the floor and sits on it.

"You should've clarified that," she says.

"I was getting to it!" We laugh for a moment. "After Arizona, I moved back home and, well, I didn't know how much my mom was struggling financially, so I helped. As I took on more responsibility, I had to take odd jobs to cover the bills. My little brother started college, and I'm helping pay for his textbooks and stuff. He got a part time job on campus, but I really want him to focus on school."

"What is he studying?"

"Nursing."

"That's honorable. Hard, I bet."

I shrug. "He's smart and tough. He'll be okay. I just want to help her in any way I can. So sometimes, I work freelance security for events, sometimes as cleanup crew. Ash and I were friends before he enlisted, and he works more..." I gesture around us. "Upscale security. He was able to get me a good offer. It'll cover some bills for a month, and I can pour the rest into savings. I'm hoping my mom can someday stand on her own again, financial independence and what not."

What I don't say out loud is that I hope my mom doesn't need me to take care of her so I can chase my dreams. I have a separate high yield savings account with the goal of being able to take a year off for writing, Harper Lee style.

"He's lucky to have you," Connie says.

It doesn't make me feel better. "I feel guilty for wishing I could do my own thing," I confess. "I'm not a good person just because I'm doing what I have to do, especially not when I spend most of my time working to do something else. I am always writing, taking notes, doing research. Every corner and crack of time I get, I take a sliver and try and create something."

"I think that just proves you are a good person, and that you're dedicated to your craft too."

"You don't get it." I toss my head back and look up at the ceiling. "Good people do good things because they want to."

"You're doing a good thing because it's the *right* thing," Connie says. "That makes it better than doing a good thing because you want some kind of credit."

"What about you?" I pick my head up and look at her. "I might not be making modern classics for the silver screen, but you're not singing either. What's up?"

Connie is quiet. "I don't want to talk about it."

I wait a minute. I want to press, but I don't want to push too hard. It's delicate. "Okay. What do you want to talk about?"

"I went no contact with my parents." Her voice is so soft, and I'm stunned. I remember when she told me about how she came out to her parents and the following screaming match. She had already moved in with Lilli, and her parents were convinced that Lilli "made her gay".

"Whenever I had a boyfriend, they would tell everyone how I was cured from homosexuality. Whenever I tried to explain bisexuality, my dad would get enraged, and my mom was dismissive. I had dated a guy for a few weeks, but it wasn't anything special, so we decided not to waste each other's time. My dad blamed my queerness. He was so mad, he beat up a trash can with his steel-toed boot."

I feel the space between us, and it's massive, a canyon. I want to jump over to her, but I can sense the physical distance is intentional, to keep our hands off each other so we can talk.

"When did you go no contact?" I ask because I can't hold her.

"Three and a half years ago."

I want to ask about her dating history since she brought it up, but I don't.

"I saw your tattoo."

I think about the ink on my chest, the sonnet it's from, and I panic. I'm not ready to talk to her about that.

"Do you have any?"

"Not yet. I think I want some, but I just can't decide."

I laugh. "What a bisexual stereotype."

We talk some more, the topics ranging from big events, like college graduations, to side jobs and anecdotes that span the last five years.

And it's just so… easy.

With Connie.

In some ways, it's like no time has passed since Arizona. Our conversations fall into an easy pattern. We're in sync. It's as if we've known each other for over half our lives.

But we haven't. We spent a week together, five years ago, plus this three week stretch of the Luxury Tour.

When the timer goes off, she gets up to start getting ready for the show tonight, and when she rises to throw the under-eye masks away, she leaves the door open.

17 – Connie – Now

It's the third and final performance of the first weekend, so Lilli and I watch the entire concert. As huge fans of Jennifer Lux, it's honestly a great time, and I'm so glad I got to experience it with Lilli. Jennifer's albums are so incredibly important to her, to both of us, really, but she takes it a step farther than me. There are times where she's gone into a Lux mode and listened exclusively to Jennifer Lux for weeks on end.

I am a Lux fan, but I like other music too. Lilli has called me out on charges of blasphemy when I've mentioned it before, and she's only mostly joking.

Jennifer's music is so universal—a modern-day Shakespeare, if Shakespeare was a lesbian. I think that's another reason why Lilli loves Jennifer Lux so much. When Lilli was twelve, she was introduced to Jennifer's *Out* album, which was unapologetically raw and beautiful. It was a big deal, because she had love songs that were written to a woman from the perspective of a woman. I know it meant a lot to me to hear that song, and I also know it was a lifeline to Lilli when she was so scared of coming out to her parents. Thankfully, her coming out was met with love and acceptance.

Wish I could say the same for mine.

As the concert ends, Jennifer Lux plays one of her dance hits, "Confetti Rain", and exits the stage.

"That was so amazing," Lilli says, her voice a little wrecked from screaming along.

"You sound awful," I laugh, but she just shrugs. "Good thing you have four days to rest before the next show."

She nods, as if that was always the plan. "I heard from some of the dancers that there's a little after party tonight."

That's news to me. I don't think anyone is buying the bit that I'm Lilli's personal assistant since they went to her directly, but also, they wouldn't know that it's only the illusion of a ruse. I've always been the one to keep Lilli on schedule and on track.

"Okay, and I'm assuming we're going to that?"

"Well, you don't have to. Ash can babysit me, which also means that if you do come out, you can have fun. You don't have to worry about me."

I think about how it might be nice to have some alone time with Eric tonight, but he hasn't made a move since Friday night when we slept together. I don't know what I expected, exactly, but maybe some validation that he wants more from me than just sex, or at least clarification that sex was the extent of our relationship.

Obviously, I haven't said anything to Lilli yet. I don't know why; I think she'd be thrilled about it, and maybe that's the problem. I don't want her to get my hopes up any higher than I will on my own. On the other hand, I don't want her to shatter my hopes either, though that seems less likely than the first. Regardless, I don't want anyone else's input right now—except for Eric. His input would actually be very helpful.

"Hey, are you coming tonight?" It's Michael. He's got that overconfident smile, the kind that tilts his head back and tugs at the corner of his mouth like a fishhook. The kind of smile that almost feels like its own red flag.

Maybe tonight, red could be my favorite color.

The party ends up being pretty fun. Jennifer, the band, the singers, and the dancers are all here, and Lilli, Jennifer, and I talk for a little while about the process of putting out an EP and a debut album.

"Connie actually writes a lot of my songs," Lilli says, and I want to kiss her; she's just given me a huge amount of credit in front of the biggest singer/songwriter of our lifetime.

"She writes too. I don't write all of them," I say, automatically deflecting. I cringe a little internally. When did it become my default to discredit myself when I'm given recognition for what I've done?

"Oh, you're Constance!" Jennifer beams, and I'm starstruck. Jennifer Lux knows my name! I keep my cool as best I can.

"I am! How'd you know?" It's a fair question, I convince myself. Everyone just knows me as Connie.

"I saw your name as a writer credit!" Seriously starstruck. *The* Jennifer Lux recognizes my name, *my* name, from a writer credit. She must have heard a song and liked it enough to look. "We'll have to get together and write something soon!"

Lilli and I agree and nod as Jennifer excuses herself to linger among her other guests.

"She likes our songs!" I cheer privately to Lilli. She does a little happy feet dance, bouncing from one foot to another quickly.

Then, all of a sudden, nothing feels real. This party, that conversation, the fact that I'm even here right now. I feel burdened and heavy, like there's nothing keeping me upright except the stubborn structure of my spine. I see the thought in my mind's eye more than I think it. I see myself dragging a stolen pencil sharpener razor across my soft unsuspecting skin, and the urge hits me a little harder than I'm used to. I wonder if the bathroom here has any nail clippers, tweezers, anything to substitute. It's been so long since I've done this, but it feels like muscle memory for my brain to jump from the urge to planning it out.

I catch myself and shut the process down. Some trains of thought need to be derailed.

Lilli excuses herself and I watch her go flirt with one of the back-up singers as Michael appears by my side.

"Glad you made it," he says.

"I was invited and had no reason to stay away," I reply. "I didn't want to be rude."

He puts a hand over his heart, as if I've wounded him. "And I thought you were here for me," he says.

I shrug. I know I decided not to sleep with this man, but maybe I'm torn.

"Let me grab you another drink," he says. "What're you having?"

"I'll get it myself, thanks," I say, "but you can go with me."

We walk over to the kitchenette, and I grab myself a fresh bottle of hard lemonade.

"Did you watch me play?" Michael asks, like a little kid asking for validation. He's putting it on like he's nervous, but I don't think this guy gets nervous when it comes to flirting. He's got all the charisma of a suburban tomcat, going around increasing the population.

"I did tonight. We watched the concert, and it was quite a production." I sip my drink. He's waiting for more. "You had some cool moments with the dramatic changes in 'Consider It', and that remix was probably my favorite part of the show tonight."

This song is normally a fast-paced dance song with a steady beat, but in the live version, they slowed it down and added some drum solos. Thematically, it worked well. The song is about burning bridges, and it was really dramatic the way it was changed up.

"Yeah, I like being able to really bring that song to life, you know?" His ego stoked, he's suddenly comfortable enough to get in my bubble. He drapes an arm around my shoulders and whispers in my ear, "Want to escape to my room for a bit? No one will miss you; we'll be back before your singer friend even notices you're gone."

I don't think he meant to insult me with the line that I'm unnoticeable and forgettable, but it's definitely giving me a bad vibe. Plue, the residual self-loathing induced by my intrusive thoughts has me wondering if I'm about to fall back into bad habits.

So much of me wants to use this man, and it's obvious he wants to use me too. He wants my body simply because he hasn't had it yet, and I want to have a reason to hate myself and a distraction from Eric.

If I say yes, then maybe I can move on, as if sex with Eric was just another fling. Maybe I'll be able to get through the next two weeks of this tour without waiting for him, without wanting him. Maybe I won't want him at all.

Except I know that with Michael, it would be just sex. Probably great sex, even, but I can't ignore the truth in my bones—everything between me and Eric has always been so much deeper than sex.

Before I can give Michael an answer, Lilli comes back around with Ash and Eric in tow. Michael doesn't react at all to their entrance; maybe he doesn't even notice, but I do. I'm acutely aware of Eric balling up his fists, his eyes narrowing in on Michael's arm around me, our bodies basically touching.

"There you are, Connie," Lilli says. "I was thinking of heading out." I can see the way she's reading the situation in her eyes: she's giving me an out if I want it, or the chance to stay. She doesn't realize Eric is close to boiling right next to her.

I remember our conversation a few days ago, how he hated the idea of Michael being around me. I hadn't made him any promises, though, and he hasn't either. If Eric wants to tie this down, put a label on whatever this is, then he needs to do it. I won't just wait around hoping to be the lucky girl who gets chosen by the guy.

So, I do something to piss him off: I turn to Michael and give him a kiss on the cheek.

"See you around," I say, careful to avoid committing to anything. I step away from him, and his hand slides down my arm until he's grasping my hand. He kisses my knuckles and reaches out his arm, holding on as long as he can until I'm out of reach.

It's cheesy and a little silly, so I giggle and say goodbye again. Ash and Lilli have turned around and started making their way out of the suite, but Eric hesitates, like he's actually weighing his options about picking a fight.

"I'm ready," I tell him to break his focus, but he doesn't look at me as he glares at Michael.

"You got some kind of problem or something?" Michael asks.

Eric huffs an exhale from his nose. "No, just getting my girl."

"Your girl?" Michael looks over at me.

"He's my security," I explain, and Michael relaxes while Eric stiffens. "Let's go."

Eric eventually turns, putting himself between me and Michael, silent most of the way to our rooms.

"Are you in middle school?" I hiss at him. "Grow the fuck up."

"I told you, I don't like him."

"Last time I checked, you don't own me. I don't have to listen to you, and you don't have to listen to me." I open my door with my room key card.

"Oh really?"

"Yep. You can go do whoever you want, because I'm not waiting for you to decide that you want me."

I move to close the door, but he stops it with his boot. "I thought you knew I wanted you already, and who is this mystery other woman I'm supposed to be hooking up with? I never knew about this."

"I can't keep doing this." I give up the battle of the door and retreat into the room. "I'm tired and a little tipsy and honestly kind of pissed at you." All of this is true. My head is already starting to ache from the booze at the party and the rollercoaster of emotions as I flop down on the bed.

Part of me expects Eric to make a pass at me, to push my limits like I suspect Michael would, but he surprises me. He grabs a water cup from the bathroom and hands it to me, pressing a kiss to my hairline.

"Get some rest, Stardust," he whispers. "I'm right here when you decide you want me."

Damn him. I don't know what just happened, but his tenderness and proximity flipped the switch on me. I want him. Now.

"Wait," I tell him as I try and pull him down to me.

"Good night, Constance."

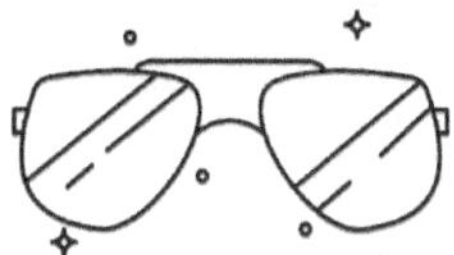

18 – Eric – Then

It was the fourth day of the festival, and I was anxious to see Connie. We didn't get to see each other at all yesterday, since we were each busy with our own workshops, but today, today was going to be a full day of hanging out.

We had been hanging out at Chris' house with a bunch of people from the festival—not quite a party, but I don't know what else to call it. I had noticed she was withdrawn throughout the day, and honestly, I couldn't figure out why, so I asked Lilli if something had happened.

"No, Connie just has low days sometimes. I never really know how to navigate them, but she wants to be alone during them, so I let her be," she said.

I heard her say that Connie wanted to be alone, and I thought about listening to her advice, but I couldn't keep myself from looking for her. I think it was unintentional, as in I never made the decision to find her. I just wandered throughout the house, subconsciously methodical in the way I started on one side of the house to the other.

Connie was nowhere inside, nor out in the backyard. I looked up at the sky growing more and more brownish gray, and I went to text her, but my phone was dead. There was a park across the street, and I finally saw her in a swing through the front window.

I didn't think twice. She seemed dimmer somehow. Maybe it was the slump in her shoulders, the way her spine curved as she lazily pushed herself back and forth in the swing. She looked defeated. My shoes made a crunching noise as I walked over to her on the wood chips, and her head snapped up before her eyes locked on mine. Recognition was the closest thing to a spark in her normally-bright eyes. I didn't know what it meant, but it scared me. I wanted to make it better, whatever it was.

"There you are!" I said, trying to brighten her spirits. She managed a small smile, and I took the victory. I sat next to her on an open swing facing the opposite direction. "Are you doing okay?"

She looked at her shoes, the toes buried in the wood chips before she shrugged and pushed the swing gently. "Yeah, I don't know. I'm just... in my own head, I guess."

Connie's voice sounded dry and small, as if she hadn't really spoken yet today. She was closed up, like a barricade holding back an onslaught of soldiers.

"Talk to me, Connie."

19 - Connie – Then

"Talk to me, Connie," Eric said.

I recognized the invitation before he vocalized it. We sat in the swings as I looked up at the grey clouds encasing us. The birds had gone into hiding. The air crackled. It was like the whole world knew I was on the edge of canceling out all my progress. Were the dark skies meant to be oppressive? Were they pushing me closer to the edge? Was nature already in mourning for the relapse I hadn't committed?

Once the words were out, they couldn't be taken back. My mind was racing. How much was too much? Did Eric care about me, or was he just enchanted by the performer? What were the tell-tale signs something was a real connection? How could you ever be sure that they love the parts of you you'd hidden away?

I weighed my options. I didn't want his pity, and I didn't want him to think I was fishing for it either. I could either annoy him, or he'd feel bad for me. Neither felt great. I could say nothing, but that wasn't a great option either. I just wanted to be honest with him. I wanted to be real, to show him all my shadows and flaws and still be enough.

I took a deep breath and let it out. Eric's eyes were still on me, waiting.

"You know how people are made up of mostly water?" I looked at him, and he had his full attention on me. I squirmed under the intensity of his gaze. "I feel like that sometimes. Like, even under still water, there is a strong current pulsing through me. I feel like a part of the ocean that has been bottled up, the water in me yearning for the vastness of its past life." I paused to see if he would ridicule me, or of he was confused, but he stayed quiet, just focused on what I was saying. He was holding space for me so I could say what I needed to. "My doctor called it Persistent Depressive Disorder. It gets better, but it also gets worse. There's not a cure; there's no end to it. It comes in waves, and I just have to live with it."

The Arizona sky was a slab of sheet metal as thunder rolled and shook through me. I leaned my head back and took in a deep breath of the thick humidity. I had no idea if my analogy made sense, but I felt a little lighter being able to put the heaviness I felt into words that were clear to me. The more ambiguous the heaviness felt, the harder it was to manage.

I could tell it was going to rain. I thought about suggesting that we go inside, find some shelter, but I also felt that desire to connect to the vastness in some way. The closest this desert could get to the ocean was in a downpour.

"I hate this," Eric said, startling me from the onset of disassociation, his voice a medicinal salve gently applied to a wound. "I wish I could take it from you. I wish I could help."

He meant it to be endearing, and it was, in a way. My heart swooned at the implication he cared enough to say anything, but I also felt like my mind had lost its footing. Does he want to take this so I'm happy, sparkling Connie all the time? Am I not good enough as I am? I remember thinking that maybe it was my fault for wearing my depression like a badge of honor, but shouldn't I be proud? Proud that I've survived all my worst days?

"It's alright," I said. Somehow, my default setting was comforting everyone else about my mental illness. "I'm still here, despite my best efforts." I gave him a smile, lightening the mood with a joke that landed like a wet towel, his eyes hard as glass.

"What do you mean?" His voice was low, almost a growl, and it set me back on the defensive.

"It's fine," I said. "I'm fine. It was months ago now, and it's not like it was a real attempt or anything. I didn't even have to go to the hospital."

"Constance."

He was still on his swing, muscles locked, and I felt ashamed. Here was a guy who watched his dad die slowly from disease beyond anyone's control or ability to heal, and I played with my life like it was trivial. I just started rambling, trying to get him to understand, praying he wouldn't hate me for the recklessness of my past.

"I couldn't go through with it. I called Lilli, and she came over and stayed with me so I wouldn't change my mind and then walked my ass to therapy." Eric's eyes were closed, and he wasn't stopping me, so I kept going. "I wasn't suicidal, I just thought about it a lot. It's intrusive, and I didn't know how to deal with it."

"But you do now?" Eric was still tightly wound, something in the furrow of his brow that showed me he was concerned, not angry. Guilt washed over me again; Eric shouldn't have to worry about a past me, a version of myself he never met.

He stood and walked over to me, lifting me out of my swing in a bear hug.

"I can't even imagine a world without you in it," he whispered into the crook of my neck as he held me.

It sounded strange, considering we had only known each other for a few days, but I felt the exact same way about him.

The tides in me swelled and, as if calling out to the molecules in the clouds, it started to rain. We started laughing, chasing each other around the playground before eventually heading back to Chris' house. We were soaking wet from rain, and there was so much said, so much more to uncover... but I felt better. Lighter. My smile didn't feel forced.

20 – Connie – Then

The rain persisted, but I felt so secure with Eric around that I didn't want to say goodbye for the night.

"Hey, Connie," Lilli said. "I kind of think I want to spend the night here. Is that okay?"

"Uh, sure."

"Do you want to take my car?"

Eric, who had been standing next to me, pitched in. "I could drive her, so you'll have your car here in the morning."

"Okay! Sounds great!" Lilli skipped back to Chris across the room and nuzzled next to her.

The drive back to the hotel was quiet but comfortable, like Eric and I were so used to each other's company that we didn't need to fill the silence. He pulled into the hotel parking lot, and I followed the sense of dread tugging at me.

"I don't really want to be alone," I said. "I don't want you to go. You can come up if you want."

His answer was a smile, his hand squeezing my thigh as he pulled into a parking space.

When we made it up to the room, he asked to use the restroom, and I took advantage of that to pick up some of Lilli's mess. There were undergarments strewn about her side of the room, butt least the bed had been recently remade. I sent out a silent thanks to housekeeping.

"It's nice in here," he said when he rejoined me.

"Yeah, it's comfortable," I agreed.

Eric walked over to me, his hands grazing up the sides of my arms softly. "What do you want to do?"

His voice was husky and low, and I felt something in me stir. He wasn't pushing or pressuring me to answer, although I knew he was waiting. I tried to find words, but it was like the connection between my brain and mouth had been severed. I rested my hands on his chest to find him solid and warm.

He looked at me like I was the night sky and he had never seen a star before, and for once, I felt like I wasn't being measured against some standard I didn't know and couldn't see. I felt adored. Purely admired.

He traced a finger along my temple and down my jaw before his whole hand cupped my jaw and pulled me in. When we kissed, I felt it all the way down in my toes like an orchestral swell. I wondered if I should give in to my own desires. It was clear what we both wanted. His kiss is sweet and gentle, delicate, and I couldn't avoid wondering if it was because I opened up about my history of self-harm. Still, it didn't feel like he found me delicate as a bomb, but rather, as precious as an antique. I didn't know why it bothered me so much.

Suddenly, I felt that familiar wave of guilt on my heart. I yanked myself back and buried my face in his neck.

"I'm sorry," I said. Sorry for how I pulled away, sorry for not being clear about my boundaries, sorry for misleading him, sorry for burdening him with my bullshit, sorry that I was about to do it again.

"Did I do something wrong?" he asked quietly, and that made me feel even more guilty.

I shook my head, the negativity in my mind growing. *You'll be nothing to him once he has you. You're making him feel bad. You're the one who invited him up here. If you're going to invite him to your room like a whore, you might as well follow through. What a pathetic little bitch.*

"Sorry, I'm spiraling." I managed to get the words out before questioning them. It was taking a gamble that Eric was the sweet guy I thought he was before my brain started painting everything in the worst light. "I can't do it."

"Do what?"

I almost died —was he really going to make me say it?

"Oh, Connie," he continued. "We don't have to have sex. We don't have to do anything. Hey," he brushed my hair back with one hand and continued holding me in the other, "I'm just lucky to be spending time with you."

I could have melted into a puddle right then, and it would've been fine. "Okay, cool."

"Can I ask something, though?" I nodded before he asked me, "Are you a virgin?"

I almost laughed. "No." I mentally kicked myself. I could have so easily blamed that as the reason I didn't want to, but no, it'd be fine. I've already been honest with him to this point. "I'm not a virgin. I used to kind of use people, though, and it's part of my self-harm addiction recovery that I abstain."

He gave me a quizzical look. Understandable. I gestured to the table and singular chair, and he took a seat as I sat cross legged on the bed.

"I grew up with a lot of purity culture influence. I would sleep with people to give myself ammunition to hate myself. I wanted sex to be something I enjoyed and did for fun, and sometimes, it was. Sometimes, though, it was just fuel for the fire of guilt and self-hatred. It was its own form of harm, and it became part of a cycle. I'd hook up with someone, and then I'd feel ashamed of it. That shame would drive me to cut more or deeper, and it just looped around. Sex. Release. Shame. Pain. Endorphins. Repeat."

Eric's eye contact was too intense for me, so I looked around the room instead of meeting his gaze. The lamp bolted onto the table behind him with its muted green base and cream lampshade was great for staring.

"I can't imagine how that was for you. I'm sorry you have all these negative associations."

"It's alright," I said. "Anyway, I decided to wait a year to sleep with anyone so I could try and break those associations."

"How long until you're at a year?"

"About a month."

Eric let out a puff of breath and shrugged. "I'll need to plan a trip out there then, if you want me to."

I couldn't stop the smile from spreading on my face, even if I wanted to.

"How about we watch a movie?" Eric asked, pointing to the television. "Get our minds off of it."

"Sure," I said as he started to flip through channels.

We caught the ending of *The Breakfast Club*, where the rebel read the note at the end of detention.

"Up next, sail the skies with *Stardust*! All movies, all day," the television announced.

I sat up. "That's my favorite movie!"

"Really? I've never seen it."

"Oh, ho, ho, buckle up, buddy! It's a masterpiece! It deserves the same level of cult praise as *The Princess Bride*."

"Strong words."

"It's tragically underrated."

He cocked an eyebrow at me. "Sounds like we need snacks."

I smiled. "Make it knock off Chinese food and you got a deal."

"Panda Express is authentic," he argued in mock offense. "It says so on their marketing paraphernalia."

"So it must be true, just like everything you see on the internet!" I quipped.

"Excuse me, the movie is starting, and I can't have you distracting me." Eric handed me his phone to order food on a delivery app. "I need to pay attention. Allegedly, this movie should rival The Princess Bride. I'm trying to impress a girl, so if you don't mind."

"Ironic, since that's the catalyst for the plot."

"Spoilers!"

The movie started, and I let it whisk me away to a world of magic and ghosts and stars that are people. Part of me longed for the fantastical world, wishing I could live there as a bard, playing in a tavern and earning my bed and breakfast with the songs I'd play. I could sing to give people space to feel what they feel. Eric watched with rapt focus, only commenting causal things regarding the physics engine of the ships, to which I simply shrugged.

"Aren't all people technically made of stardust?" Eric asked.

"Sure, but this is magical, where all stars are people."

He gave me a stunning smile that had me blushing. "You're like that star: rare and beautiful."

"Stars can't survive in a world without magic. They turn into Stardust."

"Even as dust, you're still a star, Constance." He thought for a moment. "I'm gonna call you Stardust."

"Please don't," I objected.

"You only get three objections, and you've already vetoed princess, sweetheart, and baby. Sorry, Stardust, you can't change it."

I groaned as I stood to throw away the food containers. I felt comfortable with him, but still a little nervous about the rest of the night.

"We should get some sleep," he said, and I breathed out a not-so-subtle sigh of relief.

I crawled into bed with him. It was comfortable, resting my head on his chest, both of my legs wrapped around one of his. I sleep soundly, the steady beat of his heart like a metronome.

21 – Connie – Now

This week has been exhausting, and it has only been two days. Clearly, there is no privacy on this bus, because Eric and I haven't gotten a single moment to ourselves. RVs converted into tour buses are apparently *not* meant for secret situationships. I'm trying to keep myself from making out with Eric—hell, I'm still trying to not look at him too long. Lilli's a shark; one drop of blood in the water, and she'll go into a frenzy.

We're keeping it quiet. We agreed. Sure, I came to this decision mostly on my own, but Eric agreed because I have some very good reasons.

First, I don't want Lilli all up in our business. She has enough to worry about with performing and trying to get in some hours at a recording studio.

Second, I don't know how this would affect his job. Thanks to our doorway conversation the other night, I know his mom and brother both depend on him.

Third, because I don't know what I want out of this. Situationships are hard enough as it is, let alone one with all our history. I don't want to make the same mistake. To be honest, there's no way of knowing how this could end any differently. We're the same people, after all. No one really changes that much. Although, when I think back to five years ago, I feel like a different person. Do I want a relationship or just a fling? Can Eric ever be just a fling?

These endless spirals of questioning are exactly why I don't want Lilli to know. I don't have the answers, so I'm just going to ride this out, one day at a time. Stolen moments might be all I can ever have with Eric; I'm not going to waste them.

When we stop to get gas, I have the brilliant plan to try and get some time with Eric inside, just to say hi and maybe hold his hand. We park, and I announce that I want to stretch my legs. Eric rises, picking up what I'm putting down—until Lilli agrees and comes with me, and I can't call her out on it without it seeming weird.

Ash comes with us, leaving Eric to pump the gas. I try to figure out a way to stay behind, but since going was my idea, I go. I covertly buy some Red Vines for him; I remember they're his favorite candy. While Lilli and Ash are looking at the different chip options, I check out and walk briskly back to the bus. The gas pump is on the driver's side, and the door to the bus, which is facing the storefront, is on the passenger side. Because of course it is. Nothing can be simple, can it?

I get in and go to my usual seat by the table as I open the window.

"Hey," I say.

"Hey there, Stardust."

"I got you some contraband," I say as I hand him the Red Vines.

"A woman after my heart." He's so casual, leaning up against the bus with his goofy smile, his kind eyes. No wonder this guy got me all fucked up.

"I miss you," I say before I think better of it. I'm leaning on the frame of the window now, my blonde hair flowing slightly in the light breeze. I tuck a section of it behind my ear to keep it from flying in my face.

"I've been right here," Eric says. His tone is playful, but his eyes are sober.

"But you know we can't get caught, especially you. You have more at stake than I do." He nods solemnly, and I look away from him. "When we get to the next hotel, I am going straight to bed."

"Oh, really?" He teases.

"Yep, and you'll meet me there." I look back, and his smile makes my abdomen flutter.

"Yes ma'am."

The door to the bus opens, so I hurriedly shut the window. "I'm just saying, five-star reviews mean that it's the absolute best, beyond expectations," Ash says.

Lilli vehemently disagrees. "Five stars means nothing went wrong, that my very low expectations were met."

"Do I want to know what you two are talking about?"

"Delivery food drivers."

"Oh, then I agree with Lilli," I say.

"What a shock," Ash teases.

"If you were talking about movies or something, then I'd agree with you, Ash."

"So art, which is subjective, has a harsher rating scale?" Lilli says.

"I guess when it comes to art, you can't really rate it. Any rating is indicative of a personal response and not the art itself or it's technique."

"Interesting take," Lilli says. "Almost like if someone gave you a bad review of your art, you should shake it off since art is subjective. One bad review doesn't discount all the positive ones." She's giving me a pointed look. Ash raises his eyebrows, not quite sure what turn the conversation took but realizing the train left him behind.

"Drop it," I tell Lilli as the door opens.

"Ready to get back on the road," Eric says as he joins us.

"Alright. Hey, where'd those come from?" Ash nods at the red vines in Eric's back pocket.

"Oh, uh, I ran in and got some," Eric says. Am I the only one who sees the blood tinge his face pink beneath his natural tan?

"For sure. Let's get going. Buckle up, ladies."

Eric gives me a small wink.

"What are you smiling about?" Lilli leans forward. "Are you thinking about singing with me this weekend?"

"What? No."

"Oh, okay. You should, though. I mean, obviously you should, but think about it, at least."

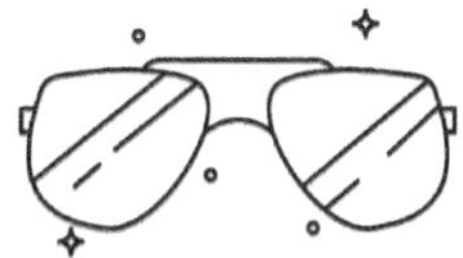

22 – Eric – Now

These bunk beds could be more comfortable. It makes sense why, on tour, Jennifer Lux opts for hotels instead. I've been awake, unable to fall asleep, when Connie gets out of her bunk. I feel like I've been tossing and turning for hours. Ash is asleep in the bunk above me, and Lilli is snoring with her feet by mine, Connie's feet were by my head. Now, she moves so slowly and quietly that if I were asleep, I'd have no way of knowing she'd moved.

She leaves the bedroom and closes the door softly behind her. I consider staying put. Would it be creepy to follow her? I'm listening, trying to hear what she's doing. Was that the front door? Where could she be going?

I roll out of my bunk, not quite as gracefully as Connie, but still quiet. I slip through the door, worried about where she could possibly be going in the middle of the night. I stop when I find her sitting cross legged on the couch, the cabinet above her open and a package of Oreos beside her. She turned on one of the lights above the couch, and she has her journal in her lap, like she was getting ready to write. Her head snaps up when she sees me: she's in the middle of taking a bite of her Oreo.

"Sorry, I didn't mean to wake you," she whispers.

"You didn't. I was already up."

Her pajama shorts and matching button up top are thin; I can see her nipples, and I force myself to look at the Oreos instead.

"Help yourself." At first, I think she means to her, but obviously, she means the cookies.

I grab one, but I don't eat it. "I can't stop thinking about you."

A seductive smile, or maybe it's a regular smile, as everything about her turns me on, tugs at her lips. "Oh yeah?" I nod as she gives a melodramatic sigh. "Too bad we have to be so quiet."

"I can be quiet," I say. "Too bad you can't be."

"Is that a challenge?"

"I'm a champion at thc quiet game."

"Oh really?"

I lean in to kiss her, and it's soft, my tongue tracing her bottom lip as she puts a hand on my chest.

"Wait," she says, and I pull back as I look into her eyes to find they're searching my face. "Are you sure you want to risk it?"

I kiss her again, less gently this time. "Constance, I would love to fuck you right here on this couch where no one would know but us." I kneel in front of her, and with all the bravado of a cartoon prince, I say, "Would you do me the honor, of letting me please you in this dark bus?"

"Quietly," she shushes me.

"I'll be very quiet, ma'am. Just do me a favor."

"What's that?"

"Do your best not to moan my name. You might wake up the sleeping beauties over there."

I grab the blanket folded on the couch and put it over us. "In case they come out here, I don't want you to be exposed."

I lay down behind her, and she rolls onto me so that she's mostly on her back. I have one arm supporting her head, and the other I wrap around her, pulling her in close as I smell her strawberry shampoo. God, I love that smell. "Never change your shampoo," I whisper.

"Did you just lose the quiet game?"

"Did we start?"

"If we did, you just lost."

"We'll start right now," I say. I emphasize the last word with a squeeze of her nipple as she gives a small gasp of surprise, and I bite her neck. Careful not to leave a mark, I focus my attention to my free hand. I squeeze the whole breast in my hand as I let each one have its own time of focus.

She laces her fingers through mine, the hand connected to the arm holding up her head. Her body is so firm and soft in all the right places.

The waistband of her little shorts stretches with ease. She reaches her hand back and grabs my package through my sweats as she pulls at the fabric, telling me my clothes are an inconvenience. With my one hand, I lower my sweats and boxer briefs. My dick is already painfully hard, and Connie's free hand drifts up my inner thigh as she grabs hold of me. Her hands are so soft, the rotation of her wrist as she strokes me up and down heaven. Her fingers circle the tip, and my cock twitches out of need. I stifle a groan, and I see her smile wickedly. Fuck, this woman is going to be the death of me. Of all my dreams of her, all the times I have pleased myself and thought of her, nothing compares. I never want this to stop, but I won't last much longer.

"Fuck, Connie."

"You lose."

"I'm not going to last, Stardust."

"Oh?" she said sinisterly, her wicked smile indulging me even further. "You better."

"Don't make me beg, Connie."

"Say please."

Damn this woman. She's got me by the balls, literally. She taunts me, going around the tip of my dick.

"Please," I say.

"Good boy. Come on me." Her shirt is unbuttoned, her torso exposed. I spill myself on her, and it's like seeing stars. She smiles at me and pulls me in for a kiss.

"Let me clean you up," I tell her, and she nods as I gingerly get up and go over to the sink. There are some wet wipes and paper towels on the counter, and I clean myself off before I go to her. I clean my mess, and she practically purrs. "Did you enjoy that?"

"Yes," I say in her ear. "Your hands are magic."

I cuddle up to her and breathe in that sweet strawberry shampoo as I kiss her a dozen times on her temple. I must have drifted off to sleep, because I'm startled awake by Connie's movement as she attempts to climb out of bed, her phone buzzing on the counter.

"No," I whisper and hold her closer.

"We can't get caught," she says. She kisses me, and I begrudgingly let her go.

"I don't want you to go."

"I won't be far," she tells me. I start to drift off again, but I hear her, and I don't know if she means for me to. "Please don't be too good to be true, Eric."

23 - Connie - Now

I'm so proud of Lilli. The show has been amazing every night, and she's been doing a great job. At first, I was a little nervous when she suggested changing the closing song each night, but it has been a hit. This is the last show until next week, and the crowds have been phenomenal. Lilli has persistently asked me to sing with her every single night, and every night, I refuse.

I try not to get too distracted. Michael keeps making eyes at me, and honestly, it's getting annoying. He seemed so chill at the party last week, but now, I feel like he's some kind of big cat, lying in wait until I show weakness.

But that's ridiculous. After her set, Lilli comes over to me, all smiles and glitter. She likes checking her phone after performances, texting her mom and sister. When we get into the dressing room, I do my personal assistant duty of making sure she hydrates.

"I can't believe we only have one more weekend of shows left," Lilli says as she starts changing her clothes.

"I know, it's going by so fast." Which is true. I haven't even dared to think beyond this tour. What would that mean for me and Eric? It's like Festival all over again: our time together has a predestined end date. The tour – at least Lilli and my reason for being here – will end soon, and then Eric and I will be forced to go our separate ways once again. Lilli and I will go back to writing songs in the apartment and trying to get a record deal. I'm grateful to know I have her in my corner, no matter what happens with Eric.

"I'm so proud of you, Lilli. I don't say it enough," I say, and she blushes slightly. "I want you to know that I'm so glad we're here together, and I look forward to where we're going." Lilli looks at me, her eyes wide with glee, a tight-lipped smile on her mouth, like she's keeping something in.

"What's up? You're being weird."

Lilli shakes her head to expel a nervous energy. "I really think you should sing with me next week."

"I don't perform anymore. I leave that to the professionals," I say, gesturing to her.

Lilli sits down in front of me, all serious business. "When are you going to start living your dream?"

"I am very happy with my life," I object. I'm taken aback by her sudden shift. We should be celebrating *her*, not squabbling about my career.

"Connie, you want more than this. I know you do." Her eyes bore into mine, and I open my mouth to speak, but there are no words. Lilli places a hand on my knee, and something about the gesture makes me want to cry. "It's time to stop living in the shadows, Connie. I want this for you, but you need to want it for yourself."

She's giving me her entire focus. "I don't know what you want from me," I say.

"I don't want anything from you. I just wish you'd take advantage of the opportunity."

Lilli sits back up and takes a drink of her water. She's still half dressed in her biker shorts and bra, no shoes, face still covered in show makeup.

"Can you focus on getting unready?" I shift gears. "I got you a new pack of facewipes."

Lilli grabs her makeup removing oil and starts rubbing it across her face, breaking down the mascara and eyeshadow. When she pulls out a facewipe, she turns to use the mirror by the sink, her back to me.

"I wanted to tell you about something," Lilli says, her focus on gently removing the mascara schmutz from under her eye. "But you have to promise not to be mad."

If I were a cat or dog, my hair would stand on end. What could it be? Was she seeing someone? Did I miss something? Maybe I've been too consumed with thoughts of Eric that I failed to notice Lilli going through something? Was it good? Or bad? Or was this her telling me Eric and I hadn't been as discreet as we thought? Did she know? Maybe I should tell her before things get out of hand.

"I need to tell you about something too," I say, trying to hide my gnawing anxiety. I should say it first, but what if she doesn't know and I blow Eric's cover? Cost him his job? "You go first," I chicken out.

"Okay, so it's kind of big, but I'm also trying not to jinx it." Lilli starts lathering her face with facewash.

"Okay?" Anticipation builds, and I wonder if she's doing this on purpose, or if she's just distracted by washing her face.

She splashes water to rinse the soap away. Grabbing a towel and patting her face dry, she turns to me. "Ripple Records sent over a contract!" She could hardly contain her excitement, and why should she? This was what we wanted, so why did I feel like the ground was caving beneath me?

"That's amazing! Why would you ask me not to be upset? This is great!" The shoe is going to drop, I know it. I can see it in the way she's wringing her hands.

"The thing is, the contract they sent was for Lillian."

I hear it, the words she's not saying. They don't want me. They don't care that half of Lillian's set was written by me. They don't care about my songs. No one cares.

My eyes can't focus on her face, so I stare at my pen cap. I pull back the tab of it so it snaps down, and Lili flinches when I let it snap. I feel bad about it, but not enough to stop. I need the outlet.

"I haven't signed it yet," Lilli says.

"Why not?"

"I sent it to my mom to look over." That makes sense—her mom is a paralegal and works on employment contracts frequently.

There's something else hidden behind her words; if she sent it to her mom already…

"You haven't signed it, but you're planning to." It's not a question, but she answers me anyway.

"Ripple Records was always the goal, and I think, maybe, this could be a good thing for both of us."

I'm silent, words not forming sentences in my head right now. I hate that she sounds like she's apologizing. I hate that there's a part of me that wants her to turn it down. I shake my head, ashamed at the thought.

"You deserve to have your own musical career outside of me," Lilli was saying. "That why I've been pushing you to perform with me; you write so many songs, and they're all so good. You should perform them. I know you have notebook after notebook filled."

My mouth is cotton. "You're assuming Ripple Records would even want me on my own. They don't even want me in tandem with you."

Lilli flushed red. "So we just need to show them that they should want you!"

"Yeah right." I sound bitter because I am, though I wish I wasn't. I want to be happy for her, so I focus on that and swallow down the resentment. It'll pass or it'll fester, but right now, it needs to take a backseat. I take a deep breath. "I am happy for you." I get up and take her hands in mine as I force myself to make eye contact.

"If your mom says the contract is good, you should sign it. You deserve this."

Tears start to well in her eyes. "You do too, though." I shrug. "No, really," she continues fiercely. "You are an amazing lyricist and an incredible singer. I hear you in the shower, while you're doing dishes. You sound amazing when you aren't even trying."

"I'm not a performer, though," I say, that same old line sounding tired and frail. "I don't have stage presence, remember?"

"Ugh!" Lilli groans in frustration. "You need to stop leaning on one piece of criticism from one guy fucking ages ago who only saw you perform on a bad day."

"I thought I did great, but it shows that I didn't. How can I trust my own interpretation of my performance?"

"Trust me."

"You're my best friend, Lillipad. You'll always tell me I did great."

"Just the truth."

"Just a skewed version of events," I counter playfully.

"You don't trust me?"

To the contrary, I think to myself. Lilli is like an extension of me, and I don't trust myself.

24 - Connie - Then

Lilli and I drove to the closest store to get swimwear for the pool party at the hotel. We weren't sure who was hosting exactly; it was more of a word-of-mouth invitation. So, naturally, when Chris asked Lilli if we'd be there, it was an automatic yes, even though we weren't prepared in any way whatsoever.

"Why do they always sell bikinis as individual pieces? I need coverage on top and below, thank you," Lilli complained as we perused the meager selection.

"Maybe to mix and match them?"

"It's a cash grab," she decided.

"Oh, definitely," I agreed. As we tried to find colors that went well together in our respective sizes, I decided to check in with her. "So, how are things going with Chris?" We moved over to the clearance rack, finding mostly cover ups and dresses left over from cooler months.

"She's so amazing." I could hear the blush in Lilli's voice. "We love a lot of the same things."

"Really? She's so… I don't know. Masculine? And you're a real girly girl."

"It's okay to say butch, Connie. Chris refers to herself as butch all the time. And yeah, we seem very yin and yang, but she's also really into skin care and hair care and accessories. It's just that her accessories are chains and belts while mine are earrings and purses."

"You do have an unhealthy purse addiction."

"They're very important to any good outfit. Besides, I need space."

"Pack rat," I teased.

"Oh! And she's so dedicated to her health and fitness. We went to the gym this morning, and she's crazy strong. And she helped me figure out some workout stuff. We ran so hard, for literally three miles. I was like, 'oh my God, I'm gonna die,' but it was so worth it."

"You hate running," I laughed. "You say it makes your face blotchy, and if you have to run, you'd rather do sprints than distance."

"Yeah, but it's good for you; like, no one likes getting vaccines but they're good for you."

"Be careful—the anti-vaxxers are going to come after you."

We laughed, but I had an unsettling feeling in my gut. Lilli liked trying new things, so I shouldn't be too worried. It wasn't like she was suddenly going skydiving or anything. There was just something off, like maybe she was trying to change herself to fit into a mold of Chris's design. Or maybe I was just overthinking it.

We made our purchases and headed back to the hotel. In my high waisted black bikini bottoms and white halter top, I was ready for the pool. I added a wrap dress with a floral white pattern on a burlap sack brown fabric. Lilli looked amazing in her low-cut, lime green one piece. She added a coverup that was some cross between a dress and a poncho.

The pool was crowded, and as I tended to do, I held hands with Lilli until we found Chris and Eric. Eric was in the deep end, shirtless and flipping his hair as he came up out of the water. Chris sat on the edge of the pool, and when she saw us, she waved us over.

"Connie!" Eric hollers. "Come on in."

"So, I kind of don't know how to swim," I admitted.

"I want to lay out on the lounge chairs," Lilli said. "Come with?" Chris got up and put her hand on the small of Lilli's back before they moved over to the chairs.

"I thought you were a camp counselor?" Eric said.

"Yeah, but never the lifeguard."

"You said your favorite part was canoe racing."

"With a life jacket on!" I stepped into the water, heading to a built-in chair in the deep end. "I'll be fine right here."

"You need to take a leap of faith, Connie," he said. "Trust me. Have I ever let you down?"

"I've known you for five days."

He smirked. "And in those five days, have I let you down?"

"No," I admitted, "but that's a small window of time. Pretty sure you need a bigger data set to form a conclusion."

"Well," Eric flashed his white teeth at me, "you'll just have to work with what you've got. And right now, you've got me."

I felt the conflict of my anxiety tensing my muscles, his presence relaxing me. My mind scrambled, looking for something to grab on to, and all I found was Eric.

"Guess I have no choice," I muttered.

"Okay then, come here." He glided closer to me, his hands on my knees. "Wrap your arms and legs around me." It seemed totally ridiculous. I'd weigh him down and we'd drown, but his smile was so endearing, and his arms felt strong and sure.

So, I did.

He carried me like a backpack, and I didn't even know how he got us over to the shallow end—probably because I had my eyes squeezed shut. "Now let's go back." Eric started swimming away from me.

"What?"

"You can't be scared of the deep end now. That's where you started." I managed a very impressive doggie paddle back to the deep end bench. "That was swimming!" Eric's smile was infectious.

"Barely."

"You got from point A to point B in water on your own. It's a win."

At this point, most of the pool had emptied. Lilli and Chris were a vivacious display of queer joy. They looked almost conspiratorial, whispering in each other's ears, unable to stop touching each other, their hands intertwined. Lilli had her free hand on their joined hands, Chris's free hand gingerly caressing Lilli's arm. The tension was palpable.

It was weird how Eric and I already felt so comfortable with each other. Since I told him I wanted to wait to have sex, he hadn't pushed me, had given me a respectful gap to the constant touching. One thing leads to another, after all. I looked back over at Chris and Lilli, and they were straight up making out... with tongue.

"They're having a good time," I joked to Eric.

"I am too," he told me, giving my hand a squeeze as he sat next to me in the water. We were weightless, my head on his shoulder as the sun set behind the trees.

"We're going to drive around," Chris called out to us.

I gave Lilli a look, making sure she was okay, but she just had stars in her eyes.

When they left, Eric and I were the only ones left at the pool as we made our way into the spa. "Do you want to talk about it?"

"Talk about what?" I said, playing dumb as he gave me a look. "Well, there are a lot of things you could be referring to. Late-stage capitalism and consumerism in a dying world. The finals performances coming up. The other night. The fact that Lilli and I are leaving tomorrow."

"Let's ignore that last one."

I shrugged. "I want to ignore all of them."

"So let's talk about something good."

"Capitalism isn't doing it for you?"

"Not tonight, sorry," he laughed, and it made my heart putter. "What are you looking forward to?"

The question caught me off guard. "All I've ever wanted to do was make music and sing to crowds who can relate to it."

"Not the fame and Tonight Show interviews?"

I laughed. "Hey, I'd love to be on a show. They seem fun."

"Is that what you're aiming for?" he asked.

"Not really aiming for it, since it's not something I can control. It's on the bucket list of things I'd like to do before I die, though."

He looked up at the sky, and I couldn't help but wonder if his dad had a bucket list, if they made it through any of those items together. What do you do when your bucket list is full of things out of your control?

25 – Eric – Then

When I got an e-mail from the judges' committee, I was nervous. A lot of work had gone into getting my short film ready for an audience, but it wasn't what I would consider my best work.

I saw the e-mail as I was walking out of the hotel after the pool party. Connie had gone up to her room, and even though I had wanted to spend another night with her, I wanted to go home. I needed to check on my cat, and I really needed some clean clothes. I'd feel better once I had a shower with my usual products. I didn't know a lot about it, but I took pride in my appearance, and I wanted to maintain healthy hair and skin.

I left the e-mail unread for the entire drive home. I pondered what it would say while I double shampooed my hair. If I was in the finals, it meant my short film would be presented to everyone again. That would be cool.

But I had this rock in my stomach about it. Was it a premonition? Was it fear? I didn't know if I'd rather get in the finals and lose or just be done and wash my hands of it.

Once my shower was over and I was in my sweats, I decided to just open the e-mail. It couldn't hurt, right?

Thank you for your submission in this year's Film Festival. We had a record number of Short Films submitted, which is very exciting for the future of cinema! Unfortunately, we can't promote every entry to the finalist level.

We regret to inform you that your project...

I closed the email and sent a text to the group chat for the actors and crew.

E: *Sorry guys, we didn't place.*

I went to call Connie and tell her the news, but she was already calling me.

"Hey," I said, already feeling lighter now that the pressure was off.

"I placed! We made it to the finals!" Connie was ecstatic, and I was so excited for her and Lilli. I wish I had been able to see their initial performance.

"Congrats, Stardust!" I cheered into the phone. I realized I'd started pacing my room, smiling like an idiot on the phone with the most amazing person I'd ever met. Something in my heart clenched—hope? Fear?

"I'll talk to you later. We're performing tomorrow, and I want to get rest," she said. She sounded just as hyped up as before as we said good night, and I started to doze off, writing a screenplay in my head.

A love story.

In the morning, I wasn't sure if it'd be better if I gave Connie space to prepare for her performance or to encourage her, so I sent her a simple good morning text, hoping her response would help indicate how to proceed. She hadn't replied until lunch time, asking me if I had time to meet up between rehearsal and sound check.

"I'm not sure why, but I feel less nervous for this than I did for the first round," Connie said as she dipped her grilled cheese into tomato soup. "I keep thinking that I should prepare for the nerves, but they just don't come."

"Maybe it's because you've already proven yourself." We sat next to each other on a booth seat because the chairs that were supposed to be on the other side were taken by another table. They were loud, singing random lines from musical theatre, but maybe Connie saw it as a welcome distraction. Part of me wanted to write it into a script, a comedy with a traveling theatre troupe where each actor performs songs from different shows to create one story.

"I haven't felt this good in a while," Connie said quietly. "I don't know. It sounds weird, but… even with my low point this week, I feel like everything is going to be okay. Like, this week has been amazing. Lilli and I were talking about this earlier. Being here, all these new professional connections… and personal ones too." She looked at me, so close, her eyes smokey and her lips so soft. I wanted to kiss her.

"I'm really glad I met you, Constance," I took her hand, "and I am so happy you're here."

I saw and felt the impact of my words as Connie let out a little breath of air yet seemed to inflate. Before I could make my move, she leaned into me, her lips on mine. My entire body was buzzing as she released me just as quickly.

A real whiplash. Connie was blushing, and she looked almost apologetic. Bashful, not regretful.

I wrapped a hand around the back of her neck and pulled her in. I kept the kiss gentle and sweet and chaste, although my mind was running a million miles beyond purity.

I was so into this girl. She was my person.

I could feel it.

26 - Connie - Then

Finals were going to be performed on a main stage. Unlike a makeshift one in a hotel conference hall, the final performances were held in the community college theatre.

With an audience.

And lighting.

At sound check, we mocked through our set, a simple two song selection, and the lighting designer set the cues for our lights. When they asked if we wanted anything specific, we explained that the first song was a dance song and to have fun with it. The second was somber, and we wanted to evoke pondering and reflection with it.

I was still giddy that Eric and I had kissed just an hour before. I wanted to have lunch with him because he calmed me, and I knew Lilli had plans with Chris. I didn't want to be alone before the sound check.

Plus, I needed to eat, and eating always felt like a social activity. Lilli seemed buzzing too when she arrived to sound check just in time for our turn. We went to the green room and waited as the audience started coming in.

"Lilli!" I said the same time she cried out "Connie!"

"You first," I said as soon as we sat down in a pair of chairs in the corner.

Lilli lifted her shirt and showed me a fresh tattoo of a barbed wire heart. The surrounding skin was raised and red, the black ink stark and scabbing beneath a square of plastic wrap.

"You got a tattoo?"

"I did! Chris got barbed wire along her sternum and her underboobs. It's very sexy." Lilli pantomimed fanning herself. "What were you going to say?"

"You won't believe what happened," I started.

Her eyes widened, and she spread her fingers out, her hands shaking like chihuahuas.

"Ohmigod, did you...?" She raised her eyebrows suggestively.

"No! No," I laughed, and she gave me a melodramatic pout. "We went to lunch, and we kissed." I felt the warmth creeping up in my cheeks.

Lilli squealed like a teenager. "I love this so much. You guys are so cute."

Something akin to fear reared its ugly head in the pit of my stomach as my mind threatened me with half sentences of incoherent despair.

He won't want you.

Won't choose you.

Not you.

You are broken.

Broken.

Broken.

Used and ugly and worthless.

You don't deserve to be here.

Unworthy.

I couldn't get it to stop. "I should go to the bathroom," I said, and I made my way along a hallway trying to find any secluded spot. I found a solitary pencil sharpener on a piano. Lucky find, or unlucky? A real question of half full or half empty.

It was both a temptation to damnation and a beacon to hope. I grabbed it with the single thought *just once* whispered in my mind like an unholy prayer.

Locking myself in the single-use bathroom, I saw my reflection in the mirror and stopped. I didn't recognize myself. Was that what my hair always looked like? How long had my skin looked deathly pale?

I heard the audience quiet as the booming voice of the organizer began the evening. I threw the pencil sharpener in the trash and leaned against the sink. Hunched over and clammy, I tried to take some deep breaths as I heard the quiet between the first and second bands. How long had I been in here?

I patted my face with the rough disposable hand towels to try and clear off the cold sweat and pinched my cheeks to bring back some color. "What's wrong with you that you have to ruin every good thing?" I asked my reflection.

Backstage was quiet as the band onstage started singing a soft ukulele ballad.

I saw Lilli in the greenroom.

"Shit, are you okay? You look like a ghost."

"Yeah, I'm just…" My throat felt tight. "I started freaking out."

Lilli's brows pinched together in concern. "About the show? We're going to be fine."

"No, I know." Since she had mentioned it, though, my wicked inner raincloud started flooding that subject with concern too. "I just… I almost…"

Her eyes widened as she leaned in close. "Are you hurt?" She put her hand to my calf; she'd seen the cuts there before.

I shook my head, and Lilli immediately relaxes and gives me a hug. "I'm proud of you."

I said nothing; I just took some deep breaths like my therapist told me to and listed out the people I love in my head. Why did I flinch when Eric's name was on that mental list? Was it some kind of premonition?

I tried to get ready for the set—just a few songs, in and out… but that fog of ambiguous guilt, shame, and fear was still weighing on my mind. I needed a release, but I couldn't cry. I couldn't self-harm because… I just couldn't give myself the option. It wasn't an option, and I held on to that.

I thought about getting my phone out and typing out my feelings into the notes app, but as I went to grab it, Lilli stood, and I realized we were on deck.

Shit. My blood was rushing in my ears as time fragmented. Suddenly, I was following Lilli on stage as I tripped on literally nothing. A few people in the audience snickered, but I couldn't see any faces in the darkness beyond the stage lights. Usually, that would be a comfort—I could pretend they weren't there or could tune them out.

But right then, it felt like I was under a microscope, my faults and failures on display. I glanced down at my calves to make sure no blood was seeping out from the bandages, but there were no bandages because I wasn't injured.

Lilli plugged her guitar in to the amp as I made my way over to the keyboard. We had the drums prerecorded, and I stepped on the pedal to start it.

It was the longest song of my life as I tried to reset my face into a mask of joy and happiness. The song was about having a great time with friends at a party at the end of summer. I was so grateful that Lilli was on the guitar to work the crowd and walk around. I just didn't have it in me.

After the song, Lilli came over to me, and I shook my head a little, indicating that I wanted to stay on keys. She nodded in understanding.

"Alright everyone, we are going to slow down a little bit," she said as she looked over at me. *Who's taking the lead?*

"This song is one I wrote," my voice is dry, "about the darkness inside us and the light worth living for. It's called 'The Depths'."

I couldn't stop the tears that blurred my vision, and as I snapped my eyes closed and sang to Eric, I knew he was out there listening. I heard Lilli singing the harmonies like a lifeline. When the song ended, I opened my eyes and saw parts of the audience had been waving their cellphone flashlights in solidarity.

I knew that, no matter what, I wanted my words to be heard. If people related to my songs, that would be enough.

27 - Connie - Now

"It's like she doesn't see my point of view!"

I'm venting to Eric, pacing the length of the tour bus. Lilli spent most of the week in a recording studio working on a demo while I've been working on more of my own songs. I just finished up a particular one about feeling betrayed; I guess that made my feelings stronger, enough to where I started complaining to Eric instead of hooking up, which is what we were originally out here to do.

"I don't care that she's signing a record deal," I continue. "I mean, I care, obviously, because I'm happy for her. It's just that I'm always the one doing the understanding, and I don't feel like I'm being understood."

Eric is silent, listening to me. I can't stop the word vomit.

"Do I think she's abandoning me? That's a strong way to word it, but a little. What am I supposed to do? Not that it's her responsibility to make my career happen for me, I know that, but she didn't even think of me, not even as an afterthought. She didn't even ask if they would consider having me come on and work with her.

"And again, I don't really blame her. I can understand how she'd get so excited about everything that she didn't stop to think. But even after I brought it up, she didn't even ask about it."

"And what did you want her to ask exactly?" Eric speaks for the first time.

"Something. If she could pick the cowriters on the album, for starters, and if so, what that looks like."

"Did you tell her that?"

I pause my pacing. I can't remember, which means I probably didn't, so I move on to other frustrations.

"I'm doing my best. Why can't she see that? She keeps trying to push me on stage, and I can't do it."

"Why not?"

"Because I stopped performing." Eric's confusion is all over his face. "Did you not know that?"

He shrugs and shifts a little in his spot on the couch. "I just figured you guys were both doing solo careers. I didn't know you gave it up."

I cross my arms. "I didn't 'give it up', I just... okay, fine, I gave it up. Thanks for making me sound like a quitter."

I sit down in the passenger seat, where Eric usually co-piolets for Ash while we're driving. It's turned around right now, facing the length of the bus.

"What if her asking you to sing is her way of trying to help you out?" he asks gently.

"Then she should say that outright, but still, it feels," I struggle for the right wording, "like a trap."

His eyebrows shoot up.

"Not like that," I say. "I just mean a trap on the cosmic scale. Lilli would never hurt me on purpose. I haven't performed since the finals at the Arts Fest."

"Five years ago?" He gives me an incredulous look. "That's insane! You were so good."

"Well, the judges told us Lilli had great stage presence, and while my performance sounded great, it was visually lacking."

"Really?" I nod, and Eric thinks for a minute. "You sang from a really vulnerable place that day. I heard it, the whole audience heard it, and you stopped because one person prefers spectacle over message?"

"You sound like Lilli," I mumble.

"Do you trust me?"

"That's a complicated question." His face is unamused, so I continue. "I do."

"Sing for me," he commands.

"What?"

"Right now, sing for me."

"I can't."

"Stardust, I have had your voice in my head since I first heard you sing. You have the kind of voice that inspires and moves people. Silencing yourself serves no one and deprives everyone."

Nerves ripple through me. My mouth feels dry, my heart constricts, and my knees are locked. I shake my head, but he grabs my hand and gives it an encouraging squeeze.

"You told me it's always scarier to perform to small, intimate groups rather than a huge crowd. You can do this. Shake it off." He shakes his whole body, and I copy him before I take a deep breath and start singing.

I sing some of Airborne, but I feel awkward singing acapella. I wince when my voice croaks on the first note.

"You've got this." Eric grins wide.

Deep breath in, and I start again. It feels better this time, but I can't look at him, so I sing to the empty space next to him. When I'm done, he claps.

"See, you did great! If you can perform to me, you can perform to a massive crowd. They'll be so lucky to hear you."

"Maybe." There are three more performances next weekend, which means I have three opportunities. "We'll see what happens."

28 - Connie - Now

I send Lilli a message that I want to talk, and she calls me immediately. "Come inside. Ash will open the door."

The hallway looks like any other office hallway, slightly dystopian and bland. I guess I understand why businesses have abstract art on their walls: it's just something to break up the monotony to keep it from looking like a cell. Or like this hallway.

Ash opens a door with a small plaque on it that reads "Studio 5".

Two people sit at the sound boards, and neither of them acknowledge me with more than a glance when I enter.

"Alright, Lillian, let's take a little break and we'll come back to this track," one of them says, their voice soft and light.

The two stand and grab a pack of cigarettes before walking out of the door.

"I'm gonna go bum a cig off one of them," Ash says. "I'm supposed to be cutting down on my nicotine," he says lifting his vape, "but man, I resisted the last two smoke breaks."

"Or you could not," Lilli chips in.

I give Eric a look; I need a minute alone with Lilli and I would prefer not to have an audience. Eric looks down at the sound board and pushes a button. "Her mic is off now," he says as he opens the door to the recording room where Lilli is.

Before I can speak, Lilli pulls me in for a hug. "I don't know what you need to talk about, but I promise to listen. I just wanted to let you know I love you, and I know things have been weird ever since I got the contract. I don't want things to be weird. You're my best friend, no matter what."

I hug her back. "I know, I'm sorry. I've been distant. I was upset, I *am* upset, but only because I'm jealous. My jealousy has nothing to do with you; it's a me issue that I'm going to work on. It shouldn't affect our friendship. You mean too much to me."

"Aww, Connie."

"And," I continue, stepping back and wringing my hands, "I think you're right."

"I agree, but what am I right about again?"

A nervous smile invades my face. "About my career."

Lilli plops down on a stool by her microphone. "Ah, yes, of course." She rolls her eyes. "Be just a tad more specific, please."

I inhale through my nose and relax my shoulders as I exhale. I can tell Lilli really doesn't see where I'm going with this. "I need to be more active in my career's growth. I need to take the reins." Lilli sits up straighter—I've caught her attention. She's watching me with bated breath. "So if it's possible, could I still…"

"Yes, oh my God, yes, yes, yes!" Lilli cuts me off and is out of her chair hugging me again.

"I don't want to intrude on your set."

"Oh nonsense," Lilli says. "It's my set, and it's not like you're going to start slandering Jennifer Lux or something."

"Do you need to check with Tops or anything?"

"Nah, I've had the sound techs set up a mic for you every show just in case. It'll all be fine."

"And you're sure?" I ask again, some scared part of me hoping for a locked door on my path forward, something beyond my control keeping me from moving ahead.

"I've *been* sure, Connie. Are you sure?"

Truthfully, I don't know, but that seems like the wrong thing to say. I was sure, *so* sure, when it was just a concept, back when this conversation was still an outline in my head, the prospect of singing on stage again nothing more than a passing idea that visited me on its way to find a performer ready to go for a ride.

I nod and swallow the lump in my throat. "No time like the moment I'm walking into," I say, quoting a Jennifer Lux song.

"And no change like the coins I spent on you!" Lilli finishes the lyric.

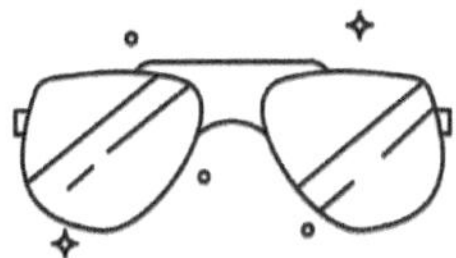

29 - Eric - Now

As it turns out, Lilli had an outfit packed and ready; I guess she always knew Connie would come around. The skirt is covered in silver sequins, each one like a shimmering coin. She adds a while bralette with a sheer, long sleeve top, and I mean sheer as in it's practically not there except to cover her in the orderly rhinestones that span the entire garment. She pairs it with lilac ankle boots with a pointed toe, completely studded with rhinestones.

Lilli's makeup and hair team take turns in a flurry of hairspray, setting spray, pinning hair back and drawing eyeliner on. It's mesmerizing, almost hypnotic.

At sound check, I force myself to my usual position in between the stage and the crowd, not wanting to leave her side. I'm already bursting with pride, and I want her to know I've got her back.

Usually, I would stand in position, wishing I could have this time backstage with Connie, but even more so tonight. I have to keep an eye on the crowd, but I wish I could dedicate my focus to watching her.

I can watch her now, though, as she sings through a verse and the chorus of a song so the audio guys can get her mic levels.

She's such a pro, no one would know it's been years since she sang for a crowd.

Part of me registers that she's jumping into the deep end. She's going from not performing to a sold-out stadium, but I have no doubt she'll capture their hearts the way her music has already has while Lilli was singing it. I'm still nervous for her though. Excited, too, but there's nerves there. I'm sure she has nerves too. I wish I could talk to her about it, wish there was something I could do.

Ash stands next to me in his usual position, his arms crossed, stance wide. "She's finally doing the damn thing." I nod as Ash takes a hit from his vape. "You guys planning on going official any time soon or what?"

I do a double take. "What?"

"Dude, I've known you for how many years now?"

I shrug in response.

"I know when you're into someone, and yeah, the history is whatever the history is, but that's in the past. Clearly, you guys are still both into each other," Ash sucks on his vape like he's an old wizard smoking a tobacco pipe.

He gives me a look, waiting for me to confirm or deny, although it's clear his mind is made up.

"If she wanted something like that, she'd tell me," I say. "Connie sets her own boundaries; I'm not going to push for more. I'm just... enjoying the time I've got."

Ash lets out a loud groan. "All of you artistic types are ridiculous." At the grimace on my face, he continues. "You're so committed to being miserable. You take the risks for your art, but not for yourself. Come on, man."

I shake my head. "You don't know what you're talking about. You're the perpetual bachelor."

"That's exactly how I know what I'm talking about. Don't be like me, dude. There was this girl. I met her out while I was stationed in Camp Pendleton, and she's the one that got away, just like you thought Connie had gotten away. Paige was really something special. She ended up getting married to some other Marine, someone she had known as a kid. I never got serious with her, even though I wanted to. If I had stopped dicking around, maybe it would've been the best thing I ever did, maybe not. Now I'll never know, though, because I let her think I wasn't serious."

"How did I not know about this?"

"How did I not know about Connie? Dude, things happen. Paige might've been the love of my life, or my soul mate is still out there somewhere. I don't know. What I do know is that you're fucking nuts about that girl up there. If I had a second chance with Paige, I'd take it in a heartbeat. Are you going to throw this opportunity away?"

Lilli puts on her stage persona as she works the crowd for a while. Her first song of the set is the same as it has been over the last several shows, but then she comes out to the front of the stage. "I have someone really special I'm going to introduce you to!" The crowd cheers. "You already know her—at least her words. She's been my songwriting partner for ages. Everyone give a big welcome to my best friend, Constance!"

Connie comes out, and I turn around to look. Ash is right next to me, keeping his eyes on the crowd. She's holding onto her microphone like a bouquet, shimmering like neon on a lake, a beautiful combination of natural beauty and fabricated glam.

"Hi everybody." Connie waves at the crowd, and they roar in response. I can feel the sound in my toes and up my body. They already love her. Of course they do. "I am so excited to be here with you guys!"

"Constance," Lillian says, "I was wondering if you'd sing a little song with me?" She nods to the guitarist, who's playing out some chords that start the song "tattoo". This is one Connie told me she helped with the bridge and verses to, but the chorus was all Lilli. It's angry, it's heartbroken, and it's still hopeful. It's looking to the future with the marks that were left behind.

I think about the tattoo I have, about how Connie might have noticed it, though if she has, she hasn't mentioned it. Sonnet 14, Shakespeare. I wonder if she knows I got it for her.

I think about Ash and Paige. This is Lilli's last show. The tour for us ends today.

What do I have to lose?

"I think I'd like to hear you sing something else for us," Lillian tells Constance before asking the crowd, "what do you guys think?" Cheers and whoops abound.

"I have something new, if you'd like to hear it," Connie says. She's asking permission, but not in the same way Lilli feeds the crowd a question. She's preparing to share something vulnerable, something untested. It's a risk, and the crowd senses her vulnerability as they cheer encouragingly. Lilli takes a seat, giving Connie the floor. Constance moves over to the piano and starts playing some chords.

"It seemed like the right thing at the time. There are some days I feel like I might end up fine. Your eyes still have the same old shine, and if it was the right time, I could be the love you find."

The lyrics hit me. Hard.

She's not looking at me; I don't even know if she's seen me looking at her.

"I swear," she sings, "there's nothing like the look on your face as I opened my soul and showed you my darkest parts. As you watched my stars fall, I thought I'd drown. In that desert, you were the force of the flash flood."

When the song ends, the crowd erupts, and I've made up my mind. I'm not going to give up.

Lilli and Connie hug, the audience cheers and cries and it's really something special.

She's really something special.

Ash and I make our way backstage to find the girls, and we find Lilli shaking.

"Oh my God, they got Connie."

Panic floods me. "What?"

"Someone tried to pull me into a cart, but Connie pushed me back and got in."

Ash speaks into his walkie. "We've got a situation. Connie has been abducted."

Abducted. The word slams into me. "What did they look like, Lilli?"

"Um, short black hair, feminine, like Alice Cullen from *Twilight*. She said she wanted to meet Jennifer Lux."

"Was she armed?"

Armed? The panic is white hot rage. *Constance.* I need to find her.

"No. I don't know." Lilli is crying now as Ash relays the information through his walkie talkie.

"Units four and six, comb the backstage corridors. Perp was driving a cart. Alone with Connie. Tops, call 9-1-1. Perp is trying to get to Lux."

"You." Ash points at me. "Stay with Lilli. Get to her dressing room."

"What? I need to find Connie," I protest. I can't just sit idlily by and wait.

"This is what I do, Eric. Trust me." He turns and leaves, Lilli shivering and sobbing behind me.

The show is halted, and Jennifer can't come out in case there's a threat to her. I can't just stand here, so I take Lilli by the hand.

When we get to the dressing room, we're met by unit three, sent to confirm Lilli's safety and monitor the corridor in case Connie or the crazy fan come this way.

Lilli is shaking on the couch while I'm pacing and resisting the urge to punch my way to Connie.

"Fuck this," I say. There's enough security to keep Lilli safe. "I have to go find her."

As soon as I open the door, though, Connie is there, wrapped in a blanket like Lilli is, clearly still in shock. There are some more security and police. There's Ash, and Tops. I can hear the concert starting in the distance—it feels like hours, but it has only been ten minutes.

I embrace her, inhaling the scent of that strawberry shampoo. "I'm okay," she says. "Just a crazy fan who wanted Jennifer."

"How did she get back here in the first place?" Tops fumes.

"She said she was a roadie with a… Michael?"

My arms tighten around Connie. That fucking prick. He put everyone in danger—he put *my girl* in danger.

The police question Lilli, then Connie, and then after, they leave with Tops walking them out.

Lilli turns to Connie with a small smile. "I'm going to change. I want to get to the hotel as soon as possible."

"Me too," Connie says. "Tops wants me to wait for her to come back, though. If you want to head over to the hotel without me, that's okay. I've got Eric."

"You're sure? I don't want to leave you. She was going to take me." Tears pool up in Lilli's eyes. "You took my place. What if something happened to you?"

"Nothing did. I'm alright, Lilli. I love you."

I watch them hug, and then I watch Lilli leave with Ash, a second car available to take us to the hotel when Tops is done with Connie.

It's misplaced from all the emotions I felt today, but I'm furious at Michael. Something much worse could've happened to Connie because of him.

When we're finally alone, Connie looks at me with a weak smile says, "Well, that was something."

30 - Connie - Now

"You should have never gone out with him," Eric simmers as he paces behind the closed door. "You know Michael is the reason she was even back here?"

"He probably didn't know," I say, unsure how we got into a conversation about Michael when I was just so relieved to be in his arms.

Can he just hold me again?

"You never should have been anywhere near him."

"You don't get to say that." I'm bitter, and maybe it's unfair, but right now, I don't give a shit.

"Why not?" Eric's anger is bubbling up. "Because you don't want to hear the truth?"

"Stop," I try to sound commanding, but my voice is weak, my mouth dry, and I hate it.

Eric doesn't notice—he's boiling over. "Because you want to settle for a jerk like Michael Soren?" I rub my temples; maybe he'll run out of steam on his own. "You can have any guy you want!"

This time, it's my turn to yell. "I know that!"

"Do you?" He marches towards me; not in threat, but with purpose. "What is it, then? The bad boy thing? Sure, Stardust, he's hot, but I don't give a fuck. Nobody gets to talk to you like that."

I scoff. "You've sure got a lot of opinions now. Where, I wonder, was all this concern for me the last five years?"

Eric straightens slightly but doesn't quite take a step back. "What do you mean?"

Seriously? The nerve. "You told me to go!" I can't believe I have to spell this out for him.

"You told me you were dating other people! That a dancer chick had asked you out repeatedly and you were considering it!"

"Eric, I wanted you to tell me not to go! To tell me to stay home and Facetime you or something. I wanted you to fight for me!"

"How was I supposed to know that?"

"I wanted you to define the relationship!" I groan and start pacing, looking anywhere but at him. "If you wanted me like I thought you did, then we would've laughed about it. Instead, you sent me off and told me to have a good time."

"You went because you wanted to go, Connie. I didn't make you."

"Because you broke my heart!" I didn't mean to say that, but it's out there now. "Because you didn't even try to fight for me. One week together, and you shattered me. I never would've believed I could be so fragile."

"Do you think I liked hurting you? You, my radiant, constant star…"

"Don't." I hold an arm out to keep him from coming closer.

He groans. "I knew you deserved so much better than me. I got home from the retreat to the apartment I was still sharing with my ex. I had to find a new place to live and a better job and figure life out all over again. That week with you was magic, but I had to focus on real life."

My voice is quiet again. "It was real to me."

"Of course it was real Connie," he sighs.

"But clearly, it didn't matter," I say. "I didn't matter. I understand, Eric. I understand that you had very important things to take care of. I understand that you were under immense stress and pressure. I'd even understand if our week at the retreat was just an exciting distraction for you. I always understand, but that does not change how it hurt me, how *you* hurt me. It still hurts, because you gave me hope, and I thought we both respected each other enough to be honest. Still, even then—hell, even now—I understand why you weren't, and I hate that I can't let myself hate you for it."

I'm right in his face, and I can see straight into his eyes, the hurt there, the same hurt he sees in mine. He's so close, and those eyes…

He's so close to me that our noses bump slightly, but neither of us turn away or step back. I want to touch his face, and it's like he feels my want radiating from me, because Eric's mouth is on mine in an instant.

It's a lustful and hungry kind of kiss, open mouthed, as if we need to devour each other in this moment. His hands grip me, one on my lower back, the other cupping my ass. My arms have wrapped around his neck, one hand clawing up his neck and into his hair.

"Fuck." He takes a step back. "I have so many things I want to say to you."

My chest heaves as I stare at him. "Say them, then."

He looks at me with those pleading puppy eyes. "First, I'm sorry. I don't know why I just blew up like that. I was so scared when they said you were in danger, and then not being able to do anything about it… I'm just so glad you're safe.

"Second, you are fucking amazing. You did a great job tonight, and I don't want to let that go. We should be celebrating.

"And third: I love you."

My mouth hangs open—he just said the L word. "Eric," I start, but the door opens, revealing Tops with none other than Jennifer Lux.

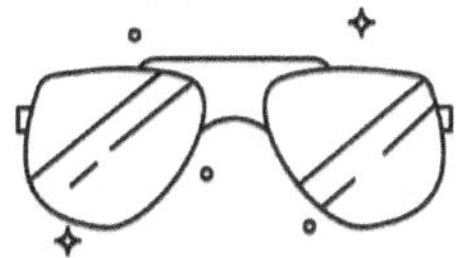

31 - Eric - Then

It was the morning I had been dreading.

I shot Chris a text to let her know I was going to say goodbye to Connie as I stopped by a coffee shop and got her a large iced coffee and a cheese Danish.

When I got to the hotel, Connie was in the lobby.

Our eyes met, and it felt like a fucking knife in the chest. She was wearing sweats and a pink racerback top, her hair pulled back in a low ponytail. I hated that she was leaving, hated that there was nothing to do about it, that I was helpless, that I couldn't guarantee we would ever see each other again.

I felt like there was so much left unsaid, and I wanted to say it all, but I couldn't find the words.

How did you tell someone you met a week ago that you want to move in? That you want to share your life with her? How did you tell the most beautiful person in the world that fairytales were written for them?

I'd never related to Romeo before, but this? This feeling of being kept from the light of your world because of physical distance… I could see how it would drive a man to recklessness.

When she nears, I pulled out the big guns, "but soft! What light through yonder elevator breaks?" It was cheesy, but it earned me a smile. Fuck, I loved that smile. What I would do to see that smile every hour of every day.

"I got you something," I held up the coffee and pastry bag.

"You're an angel," she groaned, reaching for the coffee. "I did *not* sleep well last night."

I pulled her in for a hug. "I'm sorry, Stardust."

"It's alright. I just… don't want to leave."

Lilli loaded her luggage into the car, and I noticed a bit of *something* on her face. I didn't know where Chris was, and I hoped she wouldn't ask me.

"It feels big, doesn't it?" Connie murmured to me.

"It does, but we aren't star crossed lovers. We're in the 21st century. We've got internet and cell phones and motorized transportation. If you want this like I do, we'll make it work."

"We'll find a way," she said.

"We promised each other one week of no promises. Today is day six, so tomorrow…"

"Tomorrow."

"Connie." Lilli's voice is a gentle reminder. I walked Connie to the car and opened the door.

"Don't say goodbye," she said.

"I'd never."

She sat down, and I closed the door. She waved, and so did I as the car pulled out of the parking lot.

Then, she was gone.

I stood there for a minute, unsure what to do next. I wanted to text her something so that it wouldn't feel like an ending, but I didn't want to be too clingy. My phone buzzed, and I was elated, grateful to know Connie was on the same wavelength as me. I was already smiling when I looked down to see her message.

Instead, it was Chris.

"Lilli and I are done," it says. "I made up with Gloria last night."

Was that the reason for the jealous look on Lilli's face? "Did you tell her that?" I typed back.

"Nah, man, she's gone. It was just a fling. What happens at Fest, stays at fest."

32 - Connie - Now

Jennifer Lux and I haven't spent a lot of time together, so I'm still very starstruck by being in her presence, but I try not to let it show.

This day has been insane; performing, being sort of kidnapped, that confession from Eric, and now this?

I desperately need a shower, and maybe a drink.

Jennifer is wearing her last costume from the setlist, which means that somehow, it's been nearly three hours since I was on stage.

"Hey, Constance, how are you doing?" Her voice is gentle, surprisingly enough.

Exhausted. "I'm alright."

Jennifer has a water bottle in her hands, a reusable kind with a straw, and for some reason, I'm fixated on it. I wonder absently if I've ever seen her with her hands empty before. "I am so sorry you had to go through such an ordeal today, but you handled it with grace and poise. It's irresponsible that Michael snuck someone in without going through the proper identification protocols. He'll be dealt with."

I see Eric's shoulders set. I know he wants to voice an opinion, probably to ask about more punishment, but thankfully, he keeps his mouth shut.

"Okay," I nod, because I don't know what else to say, and it feels like she's waiting on a response.

"It's my sincere hope that this doesn't discourage you from working with Ripple Records in the future," she says earnestly.

I know my mind is mush, but maybe hers is too? Is Jennifer getting me confused with Lilli?

"Lilli is still all in," I say, trying to navigate this conversation.

"That's good. You both are such great songwriters, and I was able to see your performance tonight! I really look forward to working together. I don't want to push you right now, though—you need to go rest." She takes another drink of water and smiles warmly. "Tops will give you my personal number. We'll talk later this week, okay?"

"Uh, sure." What's happening? I can't keep up.

As Jennifer Lux leaves, Tops joins us and hands some keys to Eric. "Just leave it with the valet, and I'll pick it up from there.".

"Ash and Lilli are already there," he tells her, leaning against the doorframe, Tops outside in the hall. "I think our plan is to head back tomorrow afternoon."

"Okay, good. I need to get the bus reset for the next opening act. Ash should know the process by now. Are you going to come with us for the next act?"

Eric shrugs slightly and looks back at me over his shoulder. "I go where I'm needed."

Tops pauses as she looks at Eric, then around him at me, and back up to Eric again. "Well, Ash will let you know. I think you did some good work, kid." He closes the door and lets out a long, slow exhale.

"Are you going to stay on the tour?" I ask.

His shoulders slump. "I need a nap before I make any decisions like that."

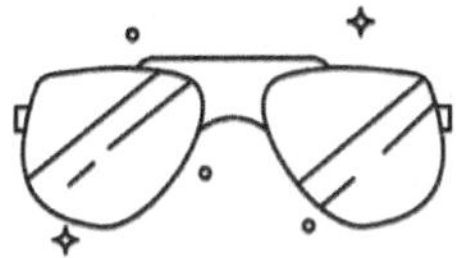

33 - Eric - Now

I slept in Connie's room that night, trash television on the hotel's wall-mounted flatscreen. I wouldn't be surprised if she's more rattled than she's letting on after the day she had yesterday.

She fell asleep with her head on my chest, her legs wrapped around my thigh. She snores a little bit with her neck at this angle, and I adjust so she can breathe easier.

Ash and I are texting as she sleeps, and Connie's phone lights up on the nightstand a few times with messages from Lilli.

Check out is 11, and it's already 9:30. If Connie has to be rushed out the door because I let her sleep in, I'm pretty sure she'll kill me.

"Hey there, Stardust," I whisper in her ear. My voice is low, and she nuzzles into me as she wakes up. Her bright eyes flutter open and lock with mine. "Good morning," I say.

"Hi," is her breathy reply. I give her a squeeze, not wanting to get up from our spot on the bed. I couldn't sleep last night, replaying the day in my head.

She never promised me anything beyond this tour, and honestly, I'm scared to ask.

Connie's phone vibrates again, and I grab it, handing it to her. She squints and reads the messages before she sits upright so fast, it makes me dizzy, and my body craves her softness back against me.

"Oh my God," she says.

I'm instantly on alert. "What happened?" I sit up, and she turns her face to me, tears welling in her eyes.

Shit, shit, shit.

"Are you okay?" I ask again. Her mouth stays shut but warbles as she nods. Something isn't right. "Connie, talk to me."

She lets out a sob. "I'm sorry," she cries. "I shouldn't be crying."

I hold her close, still very confused. "Shh, it's alright, Stardust. You're safe." I'm throwing darts in the dark. Is she having intrusive thoughts? What's happening in that mind of hers?

She's sobbing into my chest now, and oh man, I'm going to destroy whoever is making her cry. Suddenly, her shoulders shake, and I realize she's not crying—she's laughing.

"I really, I'm sorry." She pulls away and wipes the tears from her face. "I spent so long thinking I wasn't good enough." She's holding her phone to her chest like a prized memento. "I just got an email from Ripple Records."

"About what?" I ask.

Connie's beaming now. "I guess they sent a letter to my apartment the same time as Lilli's, but it was marked 'return to sender' since we weren't home. Lilli had her mail forwarded to her parents' house."

I sit there and listen, not seeing where this is going, but she seems to be getting excited.

"When they sent Lilli an offer for a recording contract, they had sent me one too! They just emailed it over to me since the snail mail one never was delivered!"

My eyes go wide. "Oh, shit! You did it!"

"I did it!" I hug her again and roll on top of her, pressing kisses into her face, her neck, her lips, her nose, her collarbone.

She's laughing and I'm so, so fucking proud.

The hotel phone is ringing, so I begrudgingly pull myself off her and pick up. "Hello?"

"Connie!" Lilli is screaming, so I hand the phone over so the girls can scream at each other over the line.

After Connie is dressed and ready, I walk her and her luggage out to the tour bus. She finds a seat on the couch inside the bus gestures for Lilli to sit with her.

"Lilli, I have to tell you something," she says. "Eric and I are..." She looks at me and takes a deep breath. "We're together."

Lilli looks between us, then over at Ash before they both start laughing so hard, Lilli forgets how to breathe.

"Sorry, sorry," Lilli says, "but I fucking called it. Ash, you owe me twenty bucks."

I look over at Ash. "You bet against us?"

Ash hands two tens over to Lilli, shaking his head. "That wasn't the bet."

"I bet Connie would tell me you guys were together before we left this hotel, and he bet that you would *propose* before we left the hotel."

"Technically, I'm the driver," Ash says. "I can wait a long time."

"Tops needs the bus," Connie mutters with a blush.

"Alright, but Eric, I'm out of twenty bucks because of you."

"Noted," I tell him.

We start driving, and Connie snuggles up against me, typing out on her notes app and sending emails to Ripple Records.

Once in a while, she looks up at me. "I love you, Eric."

I feel so whole with those four words, like every broken piece has been filled in with liquid gold, solidified, stronger than before, beautiful. Connie feels so completely like home in a way I never knew a person could be.

I kiss her hairline. "I'm never letting go of you again."

Epilogue

Connie and Eric were bringing in boxes from the rented truck. Eric didn't have too much stuff to move from his mom's house; his brother was mostly excited to have his own room.

Lilli had moved out a few days before, moving into a condo with her sister closer to Beverly Hills.

Eric had helped Connie set up their bedroom in what had been Lilli's room, the largest room in the condo. Connie's old room was going to be an office for Eric to write in, with a daybed that doubled as a couch. The downstairs room would remain a music room, and Connie had soundproofed the walls as best she could. Eric had been hired onto the writing team for a superhero movie, the third in a franchise of what would hopefully be a multiple series saga.

Connie was getting ready for the release of her debut album, *Flooded*.

"We need to get as much done as possible," she told Eric. "The listening party is tomorrow, and people will start arriving a bit before. I really want to finish setting up the house by then."

"It'll all fall into place, stardust," Eric said with a crooked smile. "You've been decorating and everything for weeks. I just have to put away these books and some clothes. That's all I have."

Connie smiled softly back. "I love that you're such a minimalist."

Eric scoffed. "Said the maximalist."

"More space for the things I like."

"Whatever makes you happy," he laughed as he planted a kiss to her forehead.

Flooded, Connie's debut album, topped the charts and was nominated for a Grammy for Album of the Year. Lilli's album, *Mindscapes*, was also nominated.

Eric's first screenplay became a blockbuster hit with an 82% on Rotten Tomatoes. They've adopted a kitten they found at a park and named her Calliope.

Connie: Hey

Eric: Hi there, Stardust.

Connie: Lol you're a nerd.

Eric: You act like this is new information.

Connie: True.

Eric: What are you up to?

Connie: just thinking about what to do with my night.

Eric: What are the options?

Connie: Well, I could stay home and order food. Or go out.

Eric: Do you have food at home?

Connie: no, I haven't had a chance to buy groceries since the trip, and Lilli went to her sister's house.

Eric: ah, so you're home alone.

Connie: I'd invite you over if we were in the same state.

Eric: *gif of a car racing*

Connie: Lol

Eric: okay, so you need to eat. Where would you go if you went out?

Connie: well, I could get drive through, or there was this dancer who offered to buy me dinner.

Eric: oh?

Connie: Yeah, I think she means on a date.

Eric: typing…

Connie: She's been asking me out for a few weeks, but she's kind of intense.

Eric: typing…

Connie: But free food is always good.

Connie: Is that bad?

Connie: I mean, I could always just order Chinese food and watch Stardust.

Eric: typing…

Eric: typing…

Eric: Maybe you should go out then. It might be fun. Do what makes you happy.

Connie: oh.

Connie: really?

Eric: If that's what you want. There's no reason not to, is there?

Connie: I guess not.

Acknowledgements

There are so many people who support and encourage me, there are so many people who assist me in creating a little idea in my head into the book your holding.

First, and always first, Jacob. Thank you for listening, for making sure I have what I need. Thank you for standing by my side as my dreams take shape. Thank you and Hazel for the times I had to disappear with my laptop for a while to work.

To my publisher - Geniece over at Birdcage Ink for always being the hype woman in the wings and helping me stay on track for my goals and deadlines.

To my editor – Alexa at The Fiction Fix. You helped polish and elevate my story to the next level.

To my cover artist – Madi at LoveLeeCreative. Working with you is such a treat, and I look forward to our next video call where you take my chicken scratch and create something beautiful for it.

To my Alpha Readers, Beta Readers, and Street Team: you guys help so much. From reading rough drafts, to sharing the word about my books online. I truly couldn't do it without you guys.

The Chaos Sisters Cohort: I'm so glad we found each other, and I love you all the way Lilli and Connie love each other. Cheers to many more books from all of us!

To everyone who has cheered me on, asked me how the writing was, and told me they were looking forward to this book – thank you!

Of course, thank you, YOU! For reading this book, for giving me a chance to tell a story. Thank you, Reader, for supporting an independent author.

Finally, again, to Jacob and Hazel. For the sacrifices you've made so I can write – I can never thank you enough.

About Stephanie Jean

HI, I'M STEPHANIE!
I'M A CALIFORNIA GIRL WHERE I LIVE WITH MY PARTNER AND OUR LITTLE GOBLIN. PISCES SUN, PISCES MOON, AND LIBRA RISING – IF YOU CARE TO KNOW.
I'M A SWIFTIE AND MY COMFORT SHOWS ARE GILMORE GIRLS AND AVATAR: THE LAST AIRBENDER.
I LOVE THEATRE AND BOOKS (OBVIOUSLY) AND THE PINK DRINK SHADE OF PINK IS MY FAVORITE COLOR.
FOLLOW ME ON BOOKSTAGRAM WHERE I POST MOST CONSISTENTLY OR MY FACEBOOK READER GROUP "STEPHANIE JEAN READER GROUP"

 @STEPHANIEJEANBOOKS

 BIRDCAGEINK.COM

Keep reading for the first chapter of

Not a Showmance
A Sapphic Romcom

Chapter One

There was a single fluorescent light flickering incessantly in the small office. "I understand, Mr. Middletop. Unfortunately, there is nothing I can do." Valerie massaged her forehead with her right hand as she adjusted the phone with her left.

"Look, I'm not trying to be an asshole," Mr. Middletop continued, even though he had very much been an asshole since calling, "but I have been very patient. I was told that your marketing team would take pictures of yesterday's event. Jorge was here, he should have them."

Valerie looked at the clock; it was still only 10:30 a.m. and she did not go to lunch until noon. "Of course," she said.

"So where are my pictures?" Mr. Middletop fumed, "Jorge was supposed to get them back to me."

"If you refer to our contract, we have a three-to-five business day turnaround for photos," she said, her words dripping like honey. "Since the event was yesterday, we will not have the photos ready at this time. If you do not receive them by the end of

the five-business day window, please call me and I will make sure
to get them to you. But for now, we just need to be patient."

"Well, you tell Jorge to call me. Or even the person he sent
yesterday."

Valerie looked through her window to Jorge's desk. He had
been at a concert last night, so she wasn't surprised when he failed
to show up today. "I will let him know to call you as soon as he's
available; is there anything else I can do for you?"

Valerie Ross worked for a marketing company named
SPRUCE, specifically in the social media department. Technically,
she had been hired to be a profile builder. A builder's job is to help
clients start their social media presence and build their own
businesses or empires or what have you. But once she started
working, she got shuffled into Reception and Editorial. While
Editorial might sound like it's a step up, it really means that Valerie
has been doomed to pick up the scraps that everyone else leaves
behind - like copying hashtags no one else bothered to, or talking to
clients when their profile builder didn't want to. Which is why she
had spent twenty minutes on the phone in her office that barely fit
her desk and a filing cabinet. She listened as Mr. Middletop went on
and on, and she tried to ignore the flickering light above her head
that was causing a migraine.

Once Mr. Middletop was appeased, she checked her email,
drafted a caption for a client with a fairy-themed bakery business,
and replaced the toner in the copy machine. *Why am I always the
one to do this? Everyone gets the notification that the toner is low.*

Her office was right next to the kitchen, so every time
someone put their leftovers in the microwave, she could smell it.
She had to remember to buy a candle or something. The four walls
of her storage closet turned office were the only walls in the
building that had never been painted. They were grey-toned with
spackle strips marking the beams in the walls. Not exactly cozy.

"What do you think about me putting up wallpaper or some
paint in my office?" Valerie had once asked a coworker during her
first few months at SPRUCE. "That could be nice," she had replied,
"but I think we are moving locations soon since we hired so many
new people." That same co-worker had quit a few weeks later to
work her dream job for a fashion magazine. Valerie had been an

employee at SPRUCE for two years now, and they still had not moved office locations, and since no one else had decorated their space, she never brought it up to her boss.

She spent a few hours after lunch making corrections to captions on posts. The amount of time she spent policing grammar was draining. She wanted to edit the photos at least; it killed her that she could not capture them. When one photographer, Chloe, decided to be a stay-at-home mother, Valerie had gotten her hopes up about finally being moved up to the position, but they hired Melissa instead. Matt attributed this to Valerie being "instrumental" to the company where she was. Flattering, but Valerie was still upset about it, and she tried not to compare herself to Melissa – who looked like she walked right out of a Cosmo magazine.

Valerie herself was not unattractive. She had an alternative style. Her wavy hair had a peek-a-boo dye job. The top was black, but underneath was bright teal, and it was chopped just above her shoulders. She had a 70's style fringe thing going on with her bangs and one small thin braid that was always in place behind her right ear. And she was curvy, but just a bit too curvy, where people stop saying curvy and start saying "bigger" in polite conversation as if to spare her feelings.

And she loved herself. But it was still hard not to wonder what it would be like to be Melissa and be able to find things that fit in any thrift store.

As if thinking about her had brought her into existence, Melissa knocked on Valerie's door. "Matt called a meeting."

"Thanks, be right there."

They met in the conference room. The conference room was a generous title for what was just a tiny room crammed with a too-large table where everyone had to struggle into their chairs. If the first people to arrive sat in the front of the room, then no one would be able to squeeze past them to the back side of the table. In short, this room was a nightmare. Valerie always tried to be one of the last people to arrive for any meetings in this room so she could slide into one of the convenient seats at the front. Sometimes she worried that people would notice her being late, but she would rather be known for being last to arrive than give everyone a show of her struggling from not being able to fit further back in the room. Especially when someone half her size couldn't fit easily.

"I have some very exciting news!" Steven from HR called the meeting to a start. "SPRUCE is expanding out of Washington to the sunny coast of Southern California!"

Co-workers began clapping. Matt and Steven were ping-ponging the presentation. Valerie tried to pay attention, but she was also working on generating hashtags for different types of accounts. "We have signed on a community theatre company in Oceanside, and Jorge will be going to build the account. Meanwhile, the finance department and management will set up an office space soon."

"There's an office already?" asked Elise, prone to blurting out questions during presentations.

"No, we are going to be shopping for one. But that's all behind the scenes. It's all going to come together," Matt replied.

Steven went on to explain that no one would be forced to relocate permanently, but if anyone was interested, to email him and they could discuss the possibility. "I can't make any promises though. It's my understanding that we would want to hire locals from the area. Keep an authentic feel in our product."

The weather in Seattle was cloudy on Valerie's drive home, but at least it wasn't raining. She hated the rain, hated how it made the lights on the street echo, hated how the windshield wipers were always either too fast or too slow, hated the feeling of water in her shoe, or a stray drop of rain sliding down her back. Thankfully, today she made her way to Tacoma without incident. The roads were clear, the ground did not reflect the lights, and her shoes remained dry until she made her way inside her apartment.

"Honey, I'm home!" she announced, flopping down on the couch. Out of the bedroom came a beautiful woman. This was Stacy Hadden, Valerie's long-term girlfriend.

"I'm actually just heading out," Stacy said.

"You are?" Valerie sat up and saw that Stacy was wearing her work clothes. As a bartender at The Last Bar, Stacy's work uniform was all black. A black T-shirt, black leggings, and black Doc Martens. The only thing that distinguished this as a work outfit was her name tag, which was shaped like a bottle of Jack Daniels on its side.

"I didn't know you had a shift. Isn't tonight date night?"

Stacy was looking in the mirror by the door, putting her chestnut hair up in a high ponytail, "Yeah, but I'm covering for Tammi." She came over and kissed Valerie on the cheek, "I'm closing, but I'll be home in the morning." Then as she walked through the front door, she called over her shoulder, "Bye!"

Valerie sank into the couch with an arm over her eyes. This was the third time in a row Stacy had canceled date night without talking about it with her first. Which was fine, she supposed. Stacy liked working because the tips were good. That was all. But for some reason, her last few paychecks hadn't been as much as they expected. "They started making us split our tips," she had said.

But Valerie knew all too well that Stacy had a history of being dishonest with romantic partners, and there was that lingering sense that something wasn't right.

Valerie and Stacy had been seeing each other for three months before she found out about Jessica. Jessica had messaged Valerie on Instagram. "I'm giving you the benefit of the doubt and assuming you didn't already know, but Stacy is a cheater. I just broke up with her. I don't want you to be blindsided like I was." As it turned out, Valerie was blindsided quite a bit. But Stacy had explained that Jessica was controlling, and manipulative. Valerie wanted to make things work. Then Stacy moved in since Jessica had kicked her out.

The last two months though, Stacy has been staying out more. Valerie has felt more like a roommate than a girlfriend. Every time they tried to plan a romantic evening or prioritize some alone time, Stacy would take off. There was less intimacy. Not just physically, but Valerie felt like they didn't really talk about anything anymore, not like they did when they had first started dating. Back then, everything was urgent, every touch and kiss felt stolen, as if they would run out of time. Maybe that was the problem? Maybe passion was finite and they used it all up too fast. Did every relationship go this way?

And what was worse, was Valerie stopped fighting. She felt that fork in the road coming, where two people in a relationship go separate ways. She tried to hit the brakes, but the split was imminent. She wondered if Stacy saw it coming too. Thoughts of where Stacy was going and who she might be with flooded Valerie's brain.

Ding ding.

Valerie tried not to think about where Stacy might be going, and who she might be with. Her phone screen showed an email from Matt.

"Had a new client sign up for a full profile build, located in Southern California. Jorge was assigned but he got Covid, so he needs to quarantine. Can you take over? Need to be on-site the day after tomorrow."

Valerie jumped up to her feet so fast, she knocked over a throw pillow. Her initial instinct was to say "Yes, I will start packing," but she had to check with Stacy first. She was not a hypocrite after all, and for all she knew, Stacy may not feel the impending fork in the road. Stacy might think everything was fine. So, Valerie grabbed her keys and ran to her car without a care for the rain that had started to pour down around her.

... Continue the story

NOT A SHOWMANCE is available everywhere books are sold.

More from Stephanie Jean

NOVELS

Not A Showmance

POETRY ANTHOLOGIES*

The Spell Jar: Book of Shadows

* one of many poets in the collection

www.ingramcontent.com/pod-product-compliance
Lightning Source LLC
Chambersburg PA
CBHW031530310726
48971CB00008B/2422